"Mr. B-Barrett," she stammered.

"Donovan," he said. "We've moved beyond formalities. Call me Donovan."

Anna swallowed nervously. "Donovan, don't worry. I would never consider that you would think of me that way. I—"

He stepped close to her. Pushing one finger beneath her chin, he bent and touched his lips to hers.

Her eyes fluttered shut. Her breath caught. She fought not to react, but his lips were so warm, his touch so compelling, she couldn't help tipping her head and kissing him back.

"Let's have honesty between us," he said. "I do desire you, and I have from the beginning, wrong though that may be."

If she were totally honest she would say that she desired him, too, but that would leave her too vulnerable. She'd been that before, and she couldn't do it again. "Don't," she said. There could be no future between someone like him and someone like her.

Dear Reader,

All right, I'll admit it. I am a sucker for a wounded hero, especially if he's a loner who tries to hide his battle scars. But I know that heroes of that type are bound to be trouble. A guy like that never follows the rules. He never does what you or the heroine wants him to do.

So when Donovan Barrett walked into my subconscious and refused to leave, I tried to ignore him. I did my best not to notice his pain or the way he fought to be tough and untouched.

Of course that didn't work. He had already won me over before I could even say no. So I allowed myself to daydream. Maybe he'd go away eventually.

No such luck. Instead, Anna Nowell stepped onto the stage. She was everything a lot of us would like to be: strong, stubborn and determined to win the key to her dreams while keeping her heart intact.

Now I had trouble. These two people were swirling around in my imagination together and neither of them wanted to get involved. They'd been hurt and needed some space. What neither of them *needed* was a romantic entanglement—especially since they both had other issues that made a relationship impossible. What neither of them *wanted* was to be attracted to the other one. And yet....

I could see the disaster approaching. A war was about to begin in my imagination. You'd think that it would be panic time, wouldn't you? Instead, I smiled. A story—a twisting, turning love story—was about to unfold, and I would have a front-row seat....

I reached for a pen.

Best wishes and happy reading,

Myrna Mackenzie

MYRNA MACKENZIE

The Maid and the Millionaire

HARLEQUIN®

TORONTO • NEW YORK • LONDON
AMSTERDAM • PARIS • SYDNEY • HAMBURG
STOCKHOLM • ATHENS • TOKYO • MILAN • MADRID
PRAGUE • WARSAW • BUDAPEST • AUCKLAND

To my mother, Virginia Mackey,
who introduced me to the joy of reading.
Thanks, Mom. You're a great role model!

ISBN-13: 978-0-373-03938-8
ISBN-10:   0-373-03938-7

THE MAID AND THE MILLIONAIRE

First North American Publication 2007.

Copyright © 2007 by Myrna Topol.

This edition published by arrangement with Harlequin Books S.A.

® and TM are trademarks of the publisher. Trademarks indicated with ® are registered in the United States Patent and Trademark Office, the Canadian Trade Marks Office and in other countries.

www.eHarlequin.com

Printed in U.S.A.

Myrna Mackenzie on
The Maid and the Millionaire

"Lake Geneva is a bit of a magical place. There's a wonderful blend of yesterday and today that appeals to the romantic in me. The historic mansions that ring the lake, the stories of the wealthy Chicago families that retreated here after the Great Chicago Fire, the beauty of the lake and the surrounding area, all combine to create a bit of a fairy-tale setting. I find something new and unique and lovely every time I'm there."

Myrna Mackenzie, an award-winning author, was recently asked what, as a child, she had wanted to grow up to be. At first she was thrown by the question. At eight, she'd been too busy playing (and reading) to think about wanting to be anything except maybe…a princess? That was it! She'd wanted to be a princess. Alhough she hasn't yet made it into the royal ranks, she's found that getting to make up stories on a day-to-day basis suits her perfectly, and is probably even more fulfilling than the princess lifestyle—even if she doesn't get to wear a tiara, silver slippers and a frothy pink dress.

Myrna lives in the Chicago area in her own little (compact) castle with her prince of a husband. They have two wonderful sons. She loves to hear from readers, and those who still love to daydream, so all other former princess wannabes (or anyone interested in contacting Myrna) can visit her online at www.myrnamackenzie.com

**Harlequin Romance®
presents a delightful story
from award-winning author**

Myrna Mackenzie

**Her rich, intense love stories
and captivating characters
will entertain you for hours!**

"Myrna Mackenzie pens an intense love story
fortified by gallant characters."
—*Romantic Times BOOKreviews*

Don't miss Myrna's next Harlequin Romance®
coming in August
Marrying Her Billionaire Boss

CHAPTER ONE

ANNA NOWELL stared at the telephone receiver she had just hung up. "Okay, don't panic," she told herself. "This is just a little bump in the road. Nothing to worry about."

But even as she whispered the words, she knew there was everything to worry about.

For two years she had been house-sitting Morning View Manor, the Lake Geneva, Wisconsin, mansion belonging to Donovan Barrett, Anna's wealthy employer and absentee owner. In all that time, Mr. Barrett had never once stepped foot on this beautiful lakefront property. With the exception of the gardeners who showed up to take care of the manicured grounds, Anna had lived here alone, playing at being lady of the manor.

Now Donovan Barrett was coming here. What was that going to mean for her?

A lump formed in Anna's throat. She knew what it meant. It meant that a house sitter was no longer necessary. She was going to lose her job.

She ran one hand over the rich golden oak of a nearby table and stroked the lush dusky-blue upholstery of a chair. Her days of pretending that she belonged here, that she had been born to privilege, were over, but not being able to pretend that this fantasy house was hers was the least of her worries.

All the time she had worked here, she had lived rent free and had been able to save a significant portion of her income. This job had paid better than most positions that were open to a woman without a university degree. Working here had not only allowed her to live a fantasy, but it had put her closer to being able to afford her dream of adopting a child.

Closer, but not close enough. She had saved some money but she could still not support another person for any significant length of time, not in the way she wanted to. And she would not bring an innocent baby into the poverty she had grown up with, the kind that had driven her father to abandon his family and had led to a painful and lonely existence for Anna. She would never subject a child to that kind of life. Not ever.

Her throat ached at the thought that she might have to postpone something she had wanted for so long, a child she could lavish with the kind of love she had never known. But truth was truth and she had grown used to meeting it head-on when she had to.

Anna swallowed. "Face it. Things have changed."

The woman on the phone had been Donovan Barrett's Chicago assistant. Tomorrow morning Mr. Barrett would move from his home base to his Lake Geneva estate.

It was less than a two-hour drive by car and yet that distance would be life-changing in so many ways.

Anna took a deep breath. She had been hired to do a job and she had done it. Donovan Barrett had needed a house sitter and now he wouldn't. It wasn't the man's fault that she wished he was staying in Chicago. Now she had to get the house ready for his arrival. She wasn't jobless yet.

"And I'm not beaten yet, either," she said, though her fear was still there. She knew little of Donovan Barrett other than what his assistant had reluctantly told her and what the area gossips had read on the Internet and shared. Born to wealth, he had been a renowned physician until the tragic accidental death of his young son. Dr. Barrett had given up his practice and become a recluse. In the eighteen months since his son's death, Donovan Barrett had become difficult. He disliked closeness; he disliked people. He craved darkness and quiet.

Anna loved light even though her upbringing had been filled with darkness. She loved conversation and music and company, perhaps because she'd had little of that in her life growing up.

She sounded like just the kind of person Mr. Barrett disliked, but…

"He'll need at least a skeleton crew," she told herself. "A cook?"

If she'd been in the mood to laugh, she would have laughed until tears rolled. She was a terrible cook.

"Okay, a maid, then." A house with ten bedrooms, six bathrooms, and a kitchen the size of a small city needed lots of cleaning.

Could she realize her dreams on a maid's pay?

Anna frowned. None of this worrying was getting her anywhere. The truth was that much of the house had been closed off for two years and now it had to be opened up, gotten ready. In less than twenty-four hours. If everything wasn't perfect, if the house didn't glow, if it didn't meet the exacting specifications that a man like Donovan Barrett was undoubtedly used to, she would appear incompetent. All hope of securing another position here would be gone. She would be jobless, homeless. She would have to dip into her savings until she found another place to work, and her hopes of becoming a mother…

Anna closed her eyes. She resisted the urge to smooth her palm over the empty place on her abdomen where other women could carry children and she took a deep, energizing breath. Self-pity wasn't allowed. It was pointless.

"Get a grip," she told herself, standing taller. "Get to work."

Maybe if she did a good job of preparing the house for its owner, she and Donovan Barrett might come to terms.

"Miracles can happen," she whispered as she set off to clean what needed cleaning, to take the dust covers off the furnishings in the rooms she had not spent much time in and to do her best to impress the man who held her fate and the fate of her unknown child in his hands.

She had to try to win the man's favor, and from what his assistant had implied, he wasn't a man particularly interested in doling out favors.

* * *

Donovan Barrett was on his way to a destiny he wasn't interested in. But he had his reasons for being in Lake Geneva, and it was here he intended to stay.

For now.

Having only visited once, he barely remembered the picturesque resort town set midway between the metropolitan areas of Chicago and Milwaukee. He did know that the lake was a summer retreat for many wealthy Chicago families and had been ever since the Civil War. His ex-wife, Cecily, was the one who had chosen the house. In retrospect, he supposed she'd wanted to get him away from his practice long enough for him to pay attention to his family, but it hadn't worked. He'd shown up once, to sign the closing papers, and had gone straight back to his patients. He'd never returned.

Driving past the shops now, he passed a long, low Frank Lloyd Wright-style building, the library, overlooking a grassy park, a beach and the east end of Geneva Lake. In the bay were small boats, sailboats with rainbow-colored sails, and a cruise ship with a paddlewheel and an open second deck filled with passengers. For a moment Donovan imagined how much Ben would have loved riding on the historic-looking vessel.

If only he'd brought his son here once. Just once. Ben had only been four years old when he died.

Donovan gripped the steering wheel and drove on toward Morning View Manor, cursing himself for all the ways he had failed his child, including not being able to save his life despite the fact that Donovan was a doctor. Rage rushed through him, and he remembered why he had come here.

Not to forget.

"That's never going to happen," he promised himself as he drove down the snaking road that led to his estate.

He would never forget Ben, but he couldn't be the man he'd been anymore. At least at Morning View he could leave his old life behind. He had to. He'd spent the first twelve months after Ben's death in a fog, but these past six months, well-meaning friends and colleagues had started to urge him to move on. Gently, at first, then more urgently. They didn't understand why he wasn't going back to his career as a successful physician or why he had to get away from a world that was a constant reminder of all he had lost.

He didn't want to hurt or disappoint those people anymore but he couldn't do what they wanted him to do.

Donovan fought the dark tide of anger that threatened to overtake him. There was no going back to his practice and there never would be. There wasn't going to be a slow slide past the pain back to meaningful relationships. His neglect had been the cause of his son's death, on more than one level. He had to live with that, but he'd do it on his own terms. He would give himself no opportunities to fail anyone else. Here, where people came to escape the reality of their worlds for brief weekends, where no one knew him, he would immerse himself in mindless diversions. He could disconnect without the sad, expectant looks from old friends.

"Here, I can pretend I never heard the words

'Hippocratic oath,' and no one will care." A grim glimmer of satisfaction greeted the thought, but Donovan had barely uttered the words when the house, a wide white building with a wall of arched windows and a fountain courtyard, came into view. Twin towers framed the house. There were five chimneys. Ten bedrooms, if he recalled the description. If he had brought Cecily and Ben here, she might have been happy. They might have stayed married. Ben wouldn't have been crossing that street at the same moment the car had gone hurtling down it.

Hot, dark agony threatened to overcome Donovan. He pulled up in front of the house with a squeal of tires and shoved his way out of the car.

Keep moving. Don't think. It was a mantra that had gotten him through many days. He angled toward the house, dug out his key and inserted it into the lock. Pulling back the wide double doors, he strode through the entrance, nearly colliding with a woman who was halfway up an old wooden ladder. An exceptionally tall ladder.

The ladder shook. Instinctively Donovan reached out. The woman swayed on her precarious perch, twisting so that her weight stopped the ominous tipping. His hand came down on the wooden frame two rungs beneath her feet.

"What in hell are you doing?" he bellowed.

He looked up into startled wide gray eyes.

"Oh, darn, I've made you angry. I didn't mean to start this way. There was just—the light needed changing." She held out the bulb. Her face was pale, and Donovan realized that he must be glowering. He recalled the explosive tone of his voice, made far worse by the disturbing thoughts he had been running from when he had opened the door.

As if he hadn't hurt enough people.

He took a step back. "I'm not angry," he said, beating back as much emotion as he could muster. He had gotten good at this skill lately. It had been necessary when friends arrived, but it was a skill he had hoped to abandon here at Morning View. He supposed he should have expected to run into someone here. He'd given his accountant free rein to make sure the place didn't fall into disrepair. He just hadn't remembered to ask the man who was working or what to expect.

It was too late to ask questions now. She was coming down the ladder. He watched as her denim-clad legs slid past him, the curve of her rear, the slope of her back. She stopped her descent when she was at eye level with him, and a brave smile lit her face. "You *are* angry," she said simply. "And why not? No doubt you weren't expecting to find someone right inside the doorway. Yet, here I am."

Yes, here she was. Donovan studied her. Her face was slightly round, slightly plump. Her hair was an unremarkable shade of brown and curved slightly, brushing her cheeks before ending just beneath her chin. She was, he supposed, a decidedly ordinary looking woman. Except for those gray eyes that seemed to stare a bit too intently, see a bit too much.

A sliver of awareness of himself as a man ran through

Donovan. Inappropriate, he thought. Meaningless. It had simply been a long time since he'd looked directly into the eyes of a woman. His reaction wasn't her fault. None of his problems were her fault.

"Who are you?" he asked, his voice more gentle this time.

Her smile grew, showing even teeth and the faint trace of a dimple in her right cheek. She pushed out one hand, the warmth of her body brushing his arm where it still rested on the frame of the ladder.

"Anna Nowell, your house sitter," she said.

He raised one brow. "I have a house sitter?"

A delicious and far from ordinary laugh slipped between her lips. "Didn't you know?"

"'Fraid not. This house and I don't have a history. My accountant handles the bills, and I let him."

"But you'll be living here now. You'll make a history. You'll need to hire more people in addition to me."

"In addition to you?" He raised a brow. She had said she was the house sitter, but now that he was here, he wouldn't need a sitter.

A faint hint of rose suffused her cheeks. "And in addition to Clyde," she added. She had a nice, low voice.

"Clyde?"

"Your gardener."

He gave a curt nod. "Any others I should know about?"

She shook her head. "Not yet. But you'll need a cook, probably a maid and a housekeeper at least."

More people. He wanted to be alone. In his penthouse in the city, he had gotten by with a cleaning service.

"I'd like to make do with a skeleton staff. I'm not used to having a lot of people around," he said.

Something flickered in her eyes. He wasn't sure what it was, but her smile faded and she looked suddenly vulnerable. Slowly she descended the last few steps of the ladder, placed the used lightbulb on one rung and looked up at him.

"I know everyone around here. I'll help you find what you need."

Somehow Donovan stopped himself from groaning. He didn't want to need anyone or anything.

"I'm sure my decision to come here caught you off guard," he said, suddenly realizing that must be true and that a job house-sitting must not pay particularly well. She probably needed the money. "I'll give you two weeks to find a new position and I'll provide a generous severance package."

Her look was so crestfallen he felt as if he'd hit her. Donovan looked to the side, but he refused to back down. The thought of he and this woman interacting on a day-to-day basis was…

"Impossible," he whispered.

"I beg your pardon?" Her voice was strained.

"Leave the ladder," he said. "I'll take care of it. And in the remaining time you're here, do not go climbing on it again. I don't want your neck broken."

I just want you gone. But he kept those words to himself as he strode past her and into the bowels of his house.

CHAPTER TWO

Two weeks. She only had two weeks to make herself indispensable to a man who just wanted to be left alone.

"So I'll become the invisible superwoman," she whispered as she laced her shoes, snatched up a clipboard and headed for the main part of the house.

For two years she had taken care of Morning View and done odd jobs on the side, but during all that time she had been the only inhabitant. Caring for this house, big as it was, hadn't been an involved process. Her needs were simple.

But Donovan Barrett was practically royalty, or at least as close to royalty as she was ever going to get. He was used to better, and she intended to give him the best.

For starters, he would need breakfast. Not exactly the job of either a house sitter, a caretaker, or a housekeeper, but for now there was no cook. While she wasn't handy with a stove, she could at least manage the basics.

She rushed down the stairs as quietly as she could just in case he was still sleeping, then picked up her pace when she heard movement, sliding into the kitchen and opening a cabinet.

For half a second, she thought about the fact that she and Donovan Barrett had slept in the same house last night. Different wings, but still more or less alone. A vision of that dark hair against a pillow hit her.

She slipped and clanged the pan in her hand against the stove.

"Stop it," she told herself. The man was miles above her in social class, wealth, education…everything, and anyway, she didn't get involved with men. She'd been foolish enough to trust her heart to at least three men, including her father. And all of them had failed her, hurt her, shredded her ego and danced on the pieces. How much more foolish to start daydreaming about someone so obviously not meant for her as her boss?

"Just make the coffee, toast and eggs, Nowell," she told herself. "Pour the orange juice." She did.

Minutes later she slid the omelet onto a Tiffany dinner plate, loaded the food upon a tray, and went in search of Donovan.

He was in the sunroom, staring out the window at the lake and the long green lawn sloping down to the water.

Anna cleared her throat.

When he turned, she tried not to notice how handsome he was. His black hair had a streak of white. His brown eyes held a touch of pain.

Stupid, she thought. Don't notice. Concentrate on staying. Adopting means jumping through hoops and having enough money. That's all that can matter. Don't try to analyze Donovan Barrett. Just get him to hire you.

"Breakfast," she said, setting the tray down on a small table flanked by white rattan chairs.

He raised one aristocratic brow. "I thought you were the house sitter, not the cook."

"House sitting involved cooking. For myself at least."

"But not for me." He gave her a long, assessing stare, and Anna felt awkward, transparent in her eagerness to please. She was thankful that she wasn't a blusher.

"You gave me two weeks, but my job of making sure the house is secured from intruders and that the pipes don't freeze in winter is essentially ended now that you're here. I'm just improvising during the interim. I can take the food away."

"No." He made a slashing movement with his hand. "You made it. It would be a shame to waste it. I'm...appreciative, but perhaps I *should* make arrangements for my meals."

Anna looked down at the slightly lopsided omelet. "It may be unattractive, but I promise you it's not poisonous."

She glanced up and thought she caught the ghost of a grin on his face. "I believe you," he said. "I'll risk it, but my point was that I didn't hire you to be a cook."

She wanted to blurt out that she could do that, but it would soon be obvious that she couldn't.

"I'll find someone," she said, her voice softer than she liked. Disappointment lanced though her. Stupid. She had known from the start that she couldn't be the cook, but with the advent of his hiring a cook, her employment options were narrowing.

"*I'll* find someone," he said. "Or at least my assistant in Chicago will. It's not your job to do extras." He stared at her, a frown forming between his eyes. Anna realized that she was twisting her hands nervously.

"Don't do that," he said. "I won't hurt you." His words were emphatic, louder than necessary.

Anna took a deep breath and raised her chin. "I never thought you would."

But he was still frowning. "I can pay you for the two weeks. You don't need to stay."

No, no, no, her mind screamed. *I can't go yet, because if I go, I can't make myself indispensable.*

She stared straight into his eyes. "I have experienced charity, Mr. Barrett, and I'll never go that route again unless I'm totally desperate. I'm not wealthy, but I'm not desperate. You said I could work for two more weeks, and I intend to work."

"It wouldn't be charity. It would be…a bonus for a job well done."

"It would be charity to me." Okay, she was pushing it here, being a bit too self-righteous when she could see that he was just trying to do the right thing. "I'd like to stay, and I intend to work at whatever tasks are necessary to the successful running of the household. I'll call your assistant and help her locate a cook."

"Ah yes, you know the town."

"I do. There's no place like it on earth, I don't believe." True, she had experienced painful moments here, but she had also found acceptance and friendship and roots. "Even though the population of Lake Geneva swells with tourists, especially on the weekends, there are really just over seven thousand people who live here year-round. They're wonderful, for the most part. I know them, and I promise you that I'll find someone talented for the position."

"I don't need much. I may not be at home all that often."

Anna was reminded once again that Donovan Barrett was from a different world. He was used to parties filled with wealthy guests, jewels, bright gowns, the scent of money, the aura of those who could have—or buy— anything they wanted.

Even babies.

The thought came unbidden. She fought her frown and kept her face impassive. It had been an unfair thought. Donovan couldn't be held responsible for her own barren state or her struggle to raise enough money to achieve her goals.

"I'll take care of everything," she promised.

She turned to go.

"Are you always this accommodating?" she heard him ask. She looked over her shoulder to see that he was frowning at his plate.

"Excuse me?"

"You've just volunteered to do extra work, and you haven't even asked for extra pay. Do you always let people take advantage of you this way?"

She didn't. It was just that she was concentrating so hard on staying here and getting paid.

"I never let people take advantage of me," she assured him, holding her head as regally as possible given the fact that she had egg yolk spilled on her apron.

His gaze locked with hers. "Good. I'm not known for my sensitive ways. I'm assuming you'll let me know if I'm too demanding an employer."

"I will." But the truth was that he couldn't demand enough of her during these next two weeks.

As for the money for extra work…

I'll cross that bridge if I manage to secure the position, she promised herself when she had left the room and returned to making a list of tasks.

She tried not to hope too hard about the future.

That kind of thing could only get a woman in trouble, and the last thing she wanted was to be in trouble with Donovan Barrett.

Donovan finished his breakfast and tried not to listen for the sound of Anna working elsewhere in the house. Even though the place was palatial, there was something about the woman that made him too aware of her. Maybe her tough I'm-a-survivor attitude, or the fact that she seemed insistent on staying and giving him his money's worth.

Or maybe the fact that now and then during that last conversation, he'd thought he saw a hint of vulnerability in her expression.

"Ridiculous," he told himself while wandering the house and getting the lay of the land. The rooms here were huge, with golden oak floors that clicked underfoot. But despite the sound of his footsteps, he could hear Anna in another room. It sounded as if she was moving furniture. He almost wanted to demand that she stop doing whatever she was doing. She was far too small to move anything heavy without hurting herself.

He clenched his hands at his side and managed to stop himself.

As he entered a long, gold and blue and white kitchen with a massive island in the center, he could hear the sound of thudding and pounding, followed by a metallic tap.

"What on earth is the woman doing?" he wondered, irritated that he was even wondering. Thudding? Pounding? That might mean messy repairs, wrestling with nails and splintering wood, getting puncture wounds, cuts and bruises.

When he heard the unmistakable sound of a hammer against wood and then a distant "ouch" he turned toward the sound and started up the stairs.

Her laughter followed, melodic feminine stuff that spun through his senses and made his blood heat.

Donovan halted. Obviously Anna wasn't hurt badly.

His concern turned to anger. Anger at himself. He had come here to disengage. He'd come here for mindless pleasure, to lose himself. Consorting with the hired help wasn't what he'd had in mind and it wasn't acceptable in the least. As the one holding the power and the money, he had to watch out for his employees and hold himself to a higher standard when dealing with them. Getting close wasn't smart and wasn't allowed.

She laughed again.

Donovan growled and turned back toward the sunroom. He pushed open the French doors and stepped onto the two-level deck, following the steps down to the lawn.

He needed to get away from Anna. Remembering her eyes, he winced. A man like him could easily hurt a woman with eyes like that.

Immediately, he realized how ridiculous his thoughts were. Just because he had hurt Cecily and Ben and others by his single-mindedness, he was starting to imagine that he was a danger to everyone. Which was idiotic. Anna Nowell wasn't even going to be here that long.

He breathed in the fresh scent of mown grass, summer blossoms and open water as he continued down the lawn toward the lake. To his left, most of the town was hidden by the curve of the shore, but on the East Coast was a huge and impressive white stone building.

Lost in his thoughts, he nearly walked into a man bending over a bed of red and yellow zinnias.

"Stone Manor," the man said.

"What?"

"That's what it's called. Stone Manor. The original owner made his fortune by buying up land on State Street after the Great Chicago Fire. I've lived here all my life but I'm still impressed whenever I look at it."

Donovan nodded. "Are you Clyde?" he asked.

The man smiled. "You must have talked to Anna."

His words sent Donovan looking over his shoulder. He could see Anna at an upstairs window. She must have finished whatever she had been doing. She was on a ladder again, dusting a high shelf.

He frowned. "I told her not to do that."

Clyde chuckled. "Telling Anna 'no' doesn't do much good. If she thinks something needs doing, she does it."

"I'm sure that's beyond the job of a house sitter."

"She wants to earn her way. You should hire her for something else."

It occurred to Donovan that his gardener was giving him advice...and that he was listening. He frowned at Clyde.

The man coughed. "Sorry. Anna's almost like a daughter. I feel protective. She needs steady, good paying work."

"I'll give her a recommendation."

"Why not keep her on here?"

Good question. He had just asked her to find him some workers. But what he had meant was find me some invisible workers, workers I won't know or care about. Not someone young with eyes that spoke to him and reminded him that he was still a man.

"I don't think that will be possible."

"That's too bad. Anna needs the money for her baby."

Donovan's breath caught and stuck in his throat. Pain lanced through him like a heated sword. "She has a child," he finally managed to say.

"She *wants* a child, and Anna will do almost anything to get one."

Donovan's chest felt tight. He was still having trouble breathing. An image of Anna begging a man to give her a child invaded his thoughts and he tried to ignore it. He fought to get back to the matter at hand.

"She needs work because she wants a child?"

"So she can *afford* to have one."

And she would risk having her heart broken, shattered, lacerated. The thoughts tumbled through Donovan's consciousness. Visions of Ben filled his head. Emotion assaulted him and he nearly stumbled.

Anna wanted a baby. She would do whatever she could to get a baby, which meant, in time, she would have one.

Being around her had just gotten more uncomfortable.

"Thank you," he said to Clyde as he turned and left. Donovan knew the man didn't know what he was being thanked for. He also knew Clyde would hate to discover what Donovan intended.

He veered toward the house, slammed through the door.

"Anna," he called, pounding up the stairs, directed by what he had seen through the window and by the sound of her humming. Her voice was low and husky.

That thought only fueled his determination. Right now they were going to end this. He would insist that she leave here.

Today.

CHAPTER THREE

ANNA was humming a favorite song. She had finished dusting the top of the high bureau and was down on her hands and knees, peering beneath the bed when she heard Donovan bellow.

She raised her head quickly, bumping it on the metal rail that held the mattress in place. Blinking back tears, she was kneeling, rubbing her head when Donovan came through the door.

"What are you doing?"

She gestured toward the bed. "Dust bunnies. You have some. I need to get rid of them."

"You need to stop climbing on ladders."

She tried not to look guilty, but didn't succeed. "You saw."

He gave her an accusing look.

"It was necessary," she argued.

"You could have fallen and hit your head. Killed yourself."

The words hung between them. Anna knew he must be thinking of his son.

"I'm always careful, and the ladder wasn't that high. Mr. Barrett, I need to do these things."

"Because you want to feel you're earning your money."

"Yes." She refused to say more.

"Clyde tells me that you want to have a baby, that you need the money to have one."

Anna blinked. "Clyde is a traitor." But she couldn't manage to sound mean. She loved Clyde like a father. "And anyway, he didn't mean…what it sounded like. I'm—" she didn't want to say it "—I'm trying to adopt a baby. I'm incapable of having my own. An accident long ago followed by surgery."

To her relief, while Donovan looked horrified, he didn't ask any questions.

But he was going to let her go. She could see it in his eyes. She knew it was because of the baby. Of course, it would hurt him to even think of children after his loss. She cared about that, she worried about that, but it didn't change her own situation.

"Please," she said. "I need the work. Let me stay. I won't mention my reasons, ever. I'll work harder than anyone you've ever known. I'll be the perfect employee. You'll get results and I'll be invisible."

She hated to beg, but Clyde was right. She needed the money and would do whatever was necessary to get it.

"Please, this job pays better than any I've ever held."

He raised his head. "I could get you work in Chicago. The pay would be good."

A deep pain went through her. She had been to Chicago once. With Brent, her fiancé, the man whose betrayal had hurt the worst. She didn't want to go back there and leave the life she had made behind. Lake Geneva was her home. She had friends who cared about her and would love her child. She was not alone.

"I don't want to leave. If I had to, I would, but I'm hoping I don't have to."

Her words were a plea.

Donovan blew out a breath. "All right, we'll try. It's obvious that you've taken good care of the house and that you're attentive to details. But when I'm home I need to be alone."

Anna gave him a grateful smile. "I'll be completely invisible."

One corner of his mouth lifted in disbelief.

"All right, I'll *try* to be invisible," she amended. Despite the hammering of her heart at Donovan's smile and his low "thank you, Anna," Anna told herself that she had gotten past the biggest hurdle.

But that was before the doorbell and the telephone started to ring over and over again. The neighborhood women had discovered that there was a new single male in town.

And all that stood between this reclusive man and them was Anna.

Donovan was in the dining room having lunch when he noticed the golden bowl in the middle of the table. Anna had obviously hired a talented cook. The food was delicious, but the bowl didn't contain food. It was filled to overflowing with envelopes.

He dragged it toward him and picked up the first one. Heavy cream-colored vellum, he held it in his hand and breathed in some expensive scent. He broke the seal.

You are cordially invited, it began.

He picked up the next and the next and the next. All invitations. All addressed to him.

He hadn't met a soul in town yet outside of Anna and Clyde and Linette, the cook. But obviously his neighbors knew that he was here. They were extending their hospitality.

For half a minute, he was tempted to pitch the whole batch in the garbage, but hadn't he come here for mindless escapism? And hadn't he been here for three days in which he'd done nothing but explore his immediate surroundings and try to ignore his—for lack of a better word—housekeeper?

That hadn't been working all that well. Donovan was constantly aware of Anna. That had to stop.

He looked at the invitations spread out before him, then picked up the first one. A family picnic, the pale script said.

"No." He placed it to one side.

The next was for a cocktail party at a neighboring mansion. "Yes." It went in another pile.

He was reaching for the third invitation when the doorbell rang. For the past couple of days Anna had been answering the door. He'd heard her light step as she moved from the stairs to the wooden floor to the marble entrance. But today she'd left a note that she had to run an errand, some piece from the hardware store that she needed to pick up.

Donovan blew out a breath and walked to the front door. He swung it back.

A woman stood on the doorstep holding a plant. When she saw him, she smiled, revealing teeth too perfect to be natural. She had blond hair that curled precisely at the curve of her jaw, flawless makeup, and she wore a tasteful gold rope at her throat that was echoed in a matching bracelet.

Donovan saw all these things in an instant, his physician's tendency to assess a situation kicking in. This woman was of his world. He had met hundreds like her over the years. Tanned, perfectly coiffed and dressed, and wearing just the right amount of scent. If she had come in a box, it would be an expensive one.

"Dana Wellinton," she said holding out one slender hand.

"Donovan Barrett," he answered automatically, shaking her hand.

"I'm your neighbor," she said. "Two lots over. I've been trying to reach you, but you haven't been home."

"I'm home now," he said, perfectly at ease. Dana Wellinton was, as he'd thought, like a copy of many other women he'd met in his lifetime. Her smile was practiced; her eyes were unreadable; her beauty was partially owed to money. She posed no threat whatsoever to his sanity.

Until she held out the plant. That's when Donovan saw that she was pregnant. A child was growing inside her, an innocent. He struggled to keep breathing normally.

It wasn't as if he hadn't seen many pregnant women

in his time. It was just that since Ben's death he hadn't been this close to one. The desire to go back in time to when Ben had still been waiting to arrive was almost overwhelming. He would do so many things differently if he could be where this woman was today.

Donovan forced himself to keep functioning. He took the plant, not looking down.

"Thank you. That's very nice of you."

"It's an orchid. Delicate. Exotic. I refused to leave it with your housekeeper."

He almost said that he didn't have a housekeeper, but for now he guessed he did.

"I'm sure Anna would have taken good care of it," he said.

"But then I wouldn't have had an excuse to meet you."

Out of the corner of his eye, he saw Anna's little white car turn into the driveway. He wondered if she had seen the woman's pregnancy or if the plant had hidden it from her as well.

Anna wanted a baby and she couldn't have one of her own. Being with pregnant women must be excruciating.

Ignoring his own reaction to the woman, he smiled at her and stepped to one side. "Come in," he said to her. "I'll ask Linette to get you something to drink. We'll sit in the sunroom."

Anna wouldn't come back there. She had, true to her promise to become invisible, been avoiding him completely. And once she was securely ensconced in another part of the house, he would politely escort his neighbor back to the door. Anna need never even see her.

* * *

Anna was pacing the floor wondering what she should do. Dana Wellinton had finally made it past the defenses she had erected and had wormed her way into Donovan's house.

The woman, who had divorced husband number two several months ago, was clearly angling for husband number three, and Donovan was a decent prospect.

"Doesn't she have any heart?" Anna muttered. Everyone had heard about Donovan's little boy and that he had still not recovered. Did Dana think her pregnancy would be a draw? A child was irreplaceable, not a toy. It was hard enough for Anna to be around the woman, knowing that Dana didn't appreciate the children she already had while other women would kill for even one baby, but for Donovan…

"I can't leave him to deal with her alone." The woman had been terribly persistent the past two times she'd come here. Donovan had probably felt that he had to be polite.

If Anna had been here, Dana would have been sent away. Taking a deep breath, Anna scooped up the first piece of paper that came her way and headed for the sunroom.

"Mr. Barrett," she said, waiting in the doorway.

Both Donovan and Dana looked up. Dana's ever present smile seemed a bit forced. "Look, Anna, he was home this time," the woman said. "I guess I got lucky at last. But then I was bound to meet him sooner or later. We *are* neighbors and fellow homeowners."

What a not-so-subtle dig, Anna thought. Clearly the hired help was being put in her place.

"Of course," Anna said. "Mr. Barrett, I hope this isn't a bad time, but I have a rather important matter I need to speak to you about." She looked down at the blank piece of paper she held in her hand. "It's about the plumbing emergency in one of the guest baths. I'm afraid it's rather urgent, but if you're busy I'll try to tend to it myself." She added that last as an afterthought. Maybe Donovan wanted to visit with Dana.

"I'm sure you can handle it, dear," Dana agreed. "Donovan and I are just getting acquainted."

But Donovan rose to his feet. "I believe in being a hands-on owner," he told Dana. "After all, I just moved to Morning View, and I need to know all its quirks and charms. These old mansions are fascinating, aren't they?"

Dana blinked. "Yes, of course, they are, but—"

"Thank you for dropping by," Donovan said. "And for the housewarming gift. I'm sure that Clyde will find a special place in the house for the orchid."

He was slowly but subtly moving Dana toward the door. The woman clearly didn't want to leave but was helpless to stop Donovan, especially when he was smiling at her as if she fascinated him.

Anna wondered if Dana did fascinate him? Did he really believe the story about the plumbing? Maybe he would be upset with her when he discovered that she had fabricated it. Perhaps her attempts to shield him had been overreaching her authority. After all, she really was just the hired help. Dana, annoying though she was, came from old money. Her ancestors had been leaders of industry. She was of Donovan's world.

As Donovan escorted Dana to the door, said his goodbyes and let her out of the house, panic began to seep through Anna. Living here for two years really had addled her brain and made her start acting like the lady of the manor when she was only here because she had begged Donovan for work.

She heard his footsteps as he turned and started heading her way, and a thousand inadequate excuses began to flit through her head.

I shouldn't have done that. I'm just the housekeeper. Turning away his neighbors wasn't what he meant when he said he wanted to be alone. He meant you, you idiot. He didn't want to be bothered by people like you.

"Interesting list you have there," she heard him say just as she felt his warm breath over her shoulder. He had stepped onto the carpeting and come up behind her while she was berating herself.

Anna tried to take a deep breath and failed as she turned to face her employer and found herself inches away and staring up into his fierce eyes.

"Now tell me, Anna, just how many of my neighbors have you turned away from my door these past few days?"

CHAPTER FOUR

DONOVAN knew what the face of guilt looked like, and Anna had guilt written in those expressive gray eyes of hers. To her credit, she didn't try to look away, but worry lines creased her brow, marring her pretty, pale skin.

"A few," she admitted. "Not many, but then…even one would be too many. I've overstepped my boundaries, haven't I?"

Her voice was stricken, penitent. She was reminding him of their employer/employee standing when only a few moments ago he had been worrying about her reaction to his pregnant visitor. Was that the way a man viewed his hired help?

No, but still…he didn't want her to feel guilty. Guilt meant pain.

"Overstepped your boundaries? That depends," he said carefully. "Why did you turn them away?"

"You said you wanted to be alone."

"I *did* say that, didn't I?"

She blinked and stood up straighter. "You don't have to let me off the hook. I made a mistake, a ridiculous one.

I should have known that when you said you wanted to be alone, you weren't referring to your neighbors but merely to those of us who share living space with you."

He did his best not to think of the fact that he and Anna lived in the same house. It wouldn't be right to allow his mind to wander down the wrong roads, wondering where she slept, what she wore, what she did with her free time. Those things were private. She might work for him but...

"Those who work for me are no less deserving of respect than anyone else," he said.

The guilt left her face. She tilted her head, a concerned look in her eyes. "Yes, but you can't think of us in the same way as your neighbors. There has to be some distance."

The faintest of smiles lifted his lips. "Giving me lessons in how to be a boss, Anna?"

Her eyes opened wide. "No, of course not. But your neighbors do occupy a different sphere than your employees. I should have asked you before assuming you meant everyone when you said you wanted to be alone."

He shook his head. "I *did* mean everyone. I needed some time to get settled in."

"But now you're settled."

"Yes, I'm settled." At least he was as settled as he was going to get.

"So I'll stop screening your visitors."

A vision of Dana with her expectant, predatory look and her pregnant belly came to him. He wasn't ready for that, and he never would be. But he wouldn't hide behind Anna.

"I'll have to meet everyone eventually. Perhaps…"

She waited.

"Perhaps you could help me sort through all those invitations. I started, but I'd appreciate your expertise."

"You'd trust me to give you advice on which parties to go to and which ones to turn down?"

He gave her a long look. "I trust you more than I trust myself. You know much more about the locals than I do, so let's at least give it a try. If there was an invitation from Dana and I asked for your thoughts…?"

She tilted her chin up. "I would advise you to stay home and read a book."

"Because?"

Anna hesitated, not sure how much she should say.

"There must be a reason," Donovan prompted.

"She wants a husband. I don't think you're looking for a wife yet."

"Very tactful," he said.

She didn't deny that she had hedged, avoiding the real issue. But the truth, the real issue, was an elephant in a closet. And it was Donovan's elephant. She wouldn't intrude by bringing up the topic of his son.

Anna waited.

Donovan's expression was grim. "Thank you, but if you're going to help me, we need to be honest." It was something he'd found to be true as a physician, and though his doctoring days were over, the basic tenet still held.

"I don't want a child ever again," he said. "You don't have to shy away from the topic. I don't." He simply shied away from *memories* of Ben as much as he could.

"All right. No pregnant women or ones with children. Women on the prowl?"

He shrugged. "I'm not looking for a wife, but I know how to keep my distance without offending." Donovan realized that he was standing very close to Anna. *Not* exactly keeping his distance. But he wouldn't be so obvious as to step away now. At least that was his reasoning for why he remained right where he was. It had nothing to do with the way her fresh womanly scent made him want to step closer still.

"No family gatherings," he added, to hide his sudden physical awareness of her. "Does that help?"

"I think so. You're looking for adults-only events. There will be plenty of those. How many do you want to accept?"

None, he wanted to say. He was content just to be standing here talking to Anna with her forthright manner and no hidden agendas. When he didn't answer, she glanced up directly into his eyes, and he could tell that she was trying to read him.

Donovan stepped away. He didn't want anyone reading his mind, and if she knew what he'd been thinking…well, the point was moot. He would monitor his thoughts more carefully from now on.

A man like him? A woman like Anna?

Improbable. Disastrous. Impossible.

"I'll accept as many invitations as I can," he said suddenly.

The more he was away from home in the next two weeks, the better off both he and Anna would be.

* * *

Anna sat at the long oak table with the golden bowl in front of her and Donovan at her side. She picked up the first invitation. Cream vellum slid through her fingers, rich and crisp to the touch. The invitations to this event probably cost more than she spent in a month on all her living expenses.

Ah, well, she couldn't eat vellum. A smile lifted Anna's lips.

"What?" Donovan's low voice slid in, that voice that reminded her of forbidden subjects. And why not? Donovan might not be looking for a bride but that didn't mean he wasn't looking for a woman.

Anna frowned. Well, he would most likely find plenty of them at one of the events represented by the cards in the bowl. "I was just admiring the…tastefulness of this invitation," she said lamely.

Donovan raised one brow. "Looks pretty much like all the other ones to me."

"That's because you're a man," Anna said, even though he had merely spoken the truth. She certainly didn't intend to tell him that she'd been thinking about what he might be planning to do with the local women.

A twinge of something that felt a bit like regret slipped through her.

Not acceptable. What he did with the local socialites was his business, not hers. He was her boss. That was all. He had asked her to do a task.

She read the invitation. It was from Kendra Williams, who was rich, beautiful and available.

Anna stared at the card.

"What do you think?" Donovan asked. "Yes or no?"

Clenching the invitation just a bit too tightly, Anna took a deep breath and placed it on the table. "Yes," she said and let out her breath.

"You seemed uncertain."

"No, I'm not. This is exactly what you wanted."

Before he could ask her any more questions, she moved quickly to the task before her, sorting the invitations efficiently into two piles. She wondered what Donovan's neighbors would think if they knew that a mere housekeeper was passing judgment on their social affairs.

Her hand shook slightly.

"Anna?"

She turned to him. He was scowling. "This was probably a mistake. I'm sure this isn't in your job description. You don't have to do this if you'd rather not."

She'd rather not. It had been easy when she was turning *everyone* away. That hadn't been judgmental. This was, and it was uncomfortable. These people might someday be potential employers. Moreover, she knew who many of them were, but she didn't really know them. They traveled in different circles than she did. Who was she to warn Donovan away from their parties?

Anna turned to tell him that he was right, this task wasn't for her. And then she remembered how he'd looked when he mentioned his son. His life had, no doubt, been a horror these past eighteen months.

It was important that he reenter the world, but she

didn't want him to be exposed to needlessly difficult or painful situations.

"I'll just look over these one last time." She reached for the yes pile and started to pick up the top one. "Just to be sure these are the ones best suited to your purpose."

Donovan looked slightly amused. "What do you perceive as my purpose?"

Anna froze in midreach. "I'm...not sure. I guess I was assuming that you wanted to ease back into the social world, to take your place again."

Donovan stared at her hand, which was still suspended. He reached out and touched her, lowering her hand to rest on the table. His fingers brushed her skin as he took the card from her.

She jerked, and her body bumped up against his. When she looked up, Donovan was closer as he stared at her intently.

"Taking my place in the world? No, I'm afraid it's nothing so lofty."

His sudden scowl caught Anna by surprise and she breathed in. The scent of his aftershave filled her senses.

"A man has to fill his days. I'm looking for mindless entertainment. That's all." He said the words as though they were a warning, then nodded toward the pile of yeses. "I assume these fit that description?"

Anna could barely think with Donovan this close. She could almost feel the echo of his words through her body. Mindless entertainment? She felt particularly mindless at the moment. If she leaned closer to him...

She took a deep breath as she realized that her thoughts were headed down a path that could only bring heartache. And worse than that, disaster. A woman in her position couldn't afford to get a reputation as someone who entertained romantic or sensual thoughts about her employer. If she did that, she'd be...unemployable.

Her dreams would be dashed forever. Panic rushed through her. What was she doing? What was she thinking?

She jerked, her chair squeaking against the oak floor.

Immediately Donovan moved away. "I'm sorry," he said, tilting his head. "I didn't mean to crowd you. I'm afraid my social skills are somewhat out of commission. That's not a good reason for startling you."

She shook her head. "You didn't. I'm fine. Really. Yes, these will do."

Getting up quickly, she moved away from the table to the sideboard.

So, Donovan was in search of mindless pleasure. She understood the why. It was a mask for his pain, a way to fill the hole that had been left by the loss of his child.

The practice of masking pain behind meaningless activity was something Anna understood. She'd learned how to do that a long time ago. She'd also learned how to fantasize, she reminded herself. About this house. And now, it seemed, about Donovan.

Anna felt sick at the thought.

"Anna, are you sure you're all right?"

"Yes. Of course."

"You've rearranged the candlesticks three times."

Anna glanced down and saw that he was right. She

was fidgeting. Because she was afraid he might have noticed her reaction to him earlier.

"That's better," she said, stepping away from the candles. Her voice sounded calm enough. She even managed a shaky smile, but inside she was appalled that he'd noticed her distress. She prayed he was unaware of where her thoughts had been heading earlier.

Those kinds of thoughts had to stop right now. Letting Donovan know that she was attracted to him in even the smallest way would be a mistake. For both of them.

He would hate himself…and he would let her go.

And she? Well, it would be the worst kind of disaster for her. Fantasizing about a man from a different social class? Very unwise. Daydreaming about a man who couldn't bear to look at a child when she hoped for one every day? A one-way trip to heartache. She almost moaned at the thought.

"Anna."

"Yes?"

Taking an energizing breath and digging for courage and control, she smiled again as she looked up at Donovan. He had risen to his feet.

"I'm sorry I made you uncomfortable," he said again, his voice even and careful. "I touched you and I can see that I've upset you. That was unforgivable. You're in my employ. I want you to feel safe. You need to know that I would never intentionally do anything that might hurt you."

Anna shook her head. "I never thought that." And she realized that she hadn't. It was her own reaction that had alarmed her. "You didn't even want me to stay. Why would you think that I would be afraid of you? I'm the one who pushed the issue of my staying. I'm just—I'm leaving because…well, I suppose because we're done here. I have work to do."

Pasting on one more brilliant smile, she waited. Thank goodness the man would soon be entering the social whirl. No doubt once Donovan took his place alongside the elite of the area, her thoughts would settle down.

I'll lose my exclusive right to him, she thought. I'll learn to do this job the right way. I will *not* fantasize about what touching Donovan would be like.

Her smile nearly faltered. "Are we done?" she managed to ask, holding her trembling hands behind her back.

Donovan frowned, still watching her closely. "We're done," he said softly.

She made her escape. What a mess! What kind of housekeeper acted like she did? None. "And ones who did probably get fired," she told herself.

Well, that wasn't going to be her. She was going to be the best housekeeper Donovan had ever known.

Two days later Donovan woke to the scent of flowers and lemon and—

"Anna," he said out loud.

A groan nearly escaped him. It was unacceptable that he had already learned her scent. What was that about?

"Inactivity," he reasoned as he got dressed and left the room. Since he'd been here he'd spent too much time in the house with no one other than his employees, and Anna was simply the employee he saw the most.

And an exemplary one at that. That lemon scent…she was polishing the furniture. He supposed she did that on a regular basis. Everything shone. The hardwood floors gleamed. Not a speck of dust or a smudge was to be found, even though this was a very large house. There was a vase of yellow roses in a cut glass vase on a sideboard in the dining room. There were flowers in almost every room.

At the moment he could hear her humming in the distance. A clank sounded, followed by an "Ow!"

Donovan frowned. He moved off in the direction of the sounds and found her tucked half-beneath a bathroom sink, a red pipe wrench almost the length of her forearm in hand.

"Anna?"

She scooted out and sat up, just missing banging her head on the hard porcelain of the sink above her.

"Yes?" Her gray eyes were wide. There was a smudge on her cheek. She looked adorable.

Donovan frowned harder still. "What are you doing?"

She looked down at the pipe wrench. "Just repairing a small plumbing problem."

"That's not necessary."

"Yes, it is. The drain was a bit slow."

"I have money. There are people called plumbers who make their living fixing drains."

She shifted her gaze to the side. "I know that, but I can do it. I have a book from the library. I've read articles on the Internet. I'm capable of handling this."

"I see." And he did. He had given her two weeks, but she needed more time, more money. For the baby she wanted.

Donovan nearly winced at that. The smartest thing to do would be to send her away, but he had promised her two weeks, and it was becoming increasingly clear that she was going to push herself to her limits in those two weeks trying to prove to him that he should keep her. Were those dark circles of exhaustion beneath her eyes?

He wanted to swear, but he didn't. As a father he had learned to watch his tongue most of the time. The thought cut into him. He ignored it. He forced himself not to think about the fact that very soon Anna might be a mother learning all she needed to know about babies instead of plumbing.

"All right," he said suddenly.

She blinked. "All right?"

"You're hired. As my housekeeper, if you want the job." He turned away, not wanting to see the eagerness in her eyes. Those eyes could unwittingly tempt a man, even a man who didn't want to be tempted.

"Yes. Thank you," she said in a quiet, grateful voice that nearly killed him. She was grateful? He didn't deserve her gratitude. She was damn good at what she did. She would be good at a lot of things. Like motherhood.

The pipe wrench clinked against metal, and he turned back. "You're hired, on one condition."

She froze, those too-innocent, grateful eyes gazing up at him. For half a second he wanted to walk back, pick her up and kiss the gratitude from those fresh berry lips, to show her that, as always, he was a bit of a selfish jerk. He would not have her thinking he was more than he was.

"I appreciate your expertise and your work ethic. You're an exemplary employee, but hire someone for the tough jobs. I don't want you hurting yourself on my watch. That's an order, Anna." He practically growled the last few words.

For a minute her lips tightened and he almost slipped up and smiled. She didn't like orders? Good. That was something he could use to keep his own inappropriate thoughts of her at bay. If she resented him, there was no danger.

He forced himself to glower at her. "I mean it."

She smiled then.

Donovan sucked in a deep breath. "What?"

"You hired me," she said simply. "I won't let you regret it."

But he already did.

CHAPTER FIVE

"OKAY, the truth has finally hit. I'm still here and by all rights I should be ecstatic, bouncing off the walls," Anna muttered to herself two days later as she prepared to make Donovan's bed. She had a good job and she didn't have to worry about losing it.

Why was there still a part of her that was worried days after she'd been given what she wanted?

Donovan had shown no signs of changing his mind. Actually, she'd hardly seen him. He'd given her the task of RSVPing to the invitations and then he had closeted himself in the library and gym. Now and then she heard the clink of weights being lifted. She tried very hard not to think about what Donovan would look like, shirtless, his muscles gleaming from the exertion.

The thought brought her up short.

Maybe ideas like that are what's worrying you, she thought. Maybe you're afraid that your gratitude to Donovan goes beyond gratitude?

"Ridiculous. He's just easy to work for," she told herself.

That must be it. He trusted her to do what needed doing and other than insisting she call in experts for the big jobs, he didn't make any rules. What woman wouldn't be overjoyed to have those kinds of workplace conditions?

Anna took a deep breath, finished the bed and headed off to do the next job on the long list of tasks she had assigned herself to do. She had more than enough to keep her mind occupied and off of her employer.

Later, however, as she worked in the big open sunroom, running a cloth over the shutters, she heard a noise, a strangled curse and all thoughts of the task at hand slipped away. Donovan had been out on the deck, reading a newspaper. Now he was on his feet, the paper on the ground, pages flying away in the breeze.

But it wasn't the escaping pages of newsprint that had caused his curse, Anna saw. His face was turned to the side as he watched something in the distance. His jaw was rigid, his hands were tight fists at his side. He held his big body so still that he might have been a statue.

She looked in the direction of his gaze. A family was on the shore path that curved around the perimeter of the twenty-one-plus miles of Lake Geneva. The path was seldom crowded, but a family out enjoying a hike here wasn't all that unusual, and Anna realized that Donovan must have surely seen other families on his section of lake frontage. It probably was painful under the best of circumstances, but this had to be worse. These people were different.

The family trailed out over the narrow path, a young

girl of about ten leading the way, followed by her mother, but it was the man and the young boy bringing up the rear that caught Anna's attention, and, she was sure, had also brought Donovan to his feet.

The child was about five or six at the most. He was painfully frail, obviously ill, and his father had stopped to lean down and speak to him, the words so soft that they didn't carry, even through the open screens of the sunroom.

The boy, however, in the way boys had, replied without regard to any listeners who might be nearby.

"I'm mostly okay," he said, when it was clear that he wasn't. "I don't want to go back inside yet. It's been so long since I've been out."

His father looked worried, uncertain, as if he'd been pushed to his limits. When he turned, Anna could see the fatigue in his expression even from here. He reached down as if to pick up the boy and carry him.

A noise on the deck, the clatter of footsteps brought Anna's attention back to Donovan. He was coming inside, and as he did, he looked at her with a dark, unreadable expression. He had shut off his emotions.

"Let them sit on the deck," was all he said. "And…if they need a ride, I would appreciate it if you would find someone to take care of that as well."

Anna nodded. "I will." She knew what he meant. There were a limited number of public access points to the shore path, and Donovan's house wasn't that close to any of them. It would be difficult for the father to carry his child the necessary distance to get back to the nearest access point.

"You don't have to handle things yourself."

She shook her head. "I want to." And there was the difference between them. Pregnant women made her uncomfortable, but children? She adored being near them, whereas they brought shadows to Donovan's eyes.

"Thank you." Donovan's voice was terse, his brows drawn together in a frown. He moved into the house.

She headed for the path. An hour later she was back at work. The parents had been grateful. They'd tried to give her money when she pulled her car up in front of the opulent resort where they were staying. When the mother had taken the children inside, the father stayed behind to talk to Anna.

"Eric has had the best doctors money can buy, and he's getting better, but it's been a tough year. He only got out of the hospital recently and we wanted to give him a special day. Thank you for sharing your deck and giving us a lift."

Anna shrugged. "I'm only the messenger. My employer owns the deck and the car that brought you here."

"I'd like to send him a thank-you."

Anna took a deep breath. She was one hundred percent certain that Donovan wouldn't want her sharing his personal information with anyone.

"I promise I'll give him your thanks," she said. She wanted to say more, but what could she say? Donovan Barrett lost a child not much older than yours? He can't be near children? Your thank-you might only remind him that he used to help children just like Eric and now he can't do it anymore?

The man looked at her as if she weren't quite as nice

as he had at first thought, but she just shook her head. "He was concerned for your family, but he's a very private man."

The dawning of understanding slid into the man's eyes. "The curse of the wealthy," he said. And Anna supposed he was partially right. She reminded herself that there were many layers that separated her from her boss, and money was one of them.

When she came back into the house, she found a grim Donovan waiting for her. "I'm sorry about that," he said.

She blinked. "It was no problem."

"You're not here to run interference for me. At least not in this way."

"I'm the housekeeper. That covers a multitude of tasks." She tried to keep her tone light and pretend she hadn't noticed Donovan's discomfort regarding the boy.

"Your job doesn't cover this, and I shouldn't have asked you to handle this situation."

"Why not? We both know that while you hired me as a housekeeper, you were doing me a favor."

He crossed his arms, raising one brow. "You're a great housekeeper."

"I don't have a clue what housekeepers are supposed to do. Well, not much of one anyway."

He glanced around. "You must be doing things right. I don't see anything wrong."

"I'm just playing things by ear." And sometimes doing it badly. She was pretty sure that most housekeepers weren't as frank with their employers as she was. "Maybe I should try wearing a uniform."

A trace of amusement crossed Donovan's lips. "If it makes you feel more official, go right ahead, but I'm fine with you as you are." He looked at her then, starting at her T-shirt and traveling down her jeans to her tennis shoes, as if he hadn't really noticed what she wore most of the time.

Awareness ripped through Anna, and her T-shirt suddenly felt too tight. She glanced down at the Live For Today emblazoned across her chest in blazing hot-pink.

"This is probably not very professional," she admitted.

But when she looked up and saw that the shadows had flown from his eyes, her concern about her clothing fled.

"I like the sentiment," he said. "It suits you." He started to turn away, then turned back, his lips tight.

"They're all right?"

She didn't have to ask who "they" were. "Yes," she said, "and the little boy's health is improving. His father sends his thanks."

"He should have been thanking *you*."

"He did."

"Good." Donovan's voice was clipped. He was studying her intently. Anna felt too aware of herself in a way she never had before.

Somewhere in the house, a clock chimed softly. Six o'clock. Like Cinderella startled by the knowledge that she had to run, Anna realized that she had been staring into her boss's eyes for too long. She also realized something else.

"You're due at the Williams's party in an hour."

Donovan frowned and swore.

Anna blinked. Donovan never swore.

"I'm sorry," he said. "I'd forgotten about the party."

She shook her head, confused. "You don't sound as if you really want to go."

He looked into her eyes and her stomach flipped over. Darn this man for making her suddenly wake up to her own femininity. She didn't want a man. She certainly couldn't want this man. She had heart-deep dreams that clashed with everything Donovan was and would be, and even if that weren't true...

She ran her fingers purposely across the rip in the thigh of her jeans. She wasn't wearing them to be fashionable but because she couldn't afford to buy new ones and she hadn't had time to patch these yet. The women Donovan would spend his time with tonight would never be in that kind of situation. Someday she might be cleaning the house of one of those ladies.

Donovan was studying her carefully. She prayed that he couldn't read her thoughts or know how much he affected her.

"I want to go to the party," he said. "It's why I came here. To play."

Anna nodded. "Then you'd better go play. You'd better get ready. I'll just get back to what I was doing."

Slowly, he shook his head. "No."

"No?" She frowned, not sure what he meant.

"It's six o'clock. Go home, Anna."

But they both knew that she lived here. She would be here when he left and she would be here when he got back.

And in the hours in between? she asked herself.

She would *not* think about what he was doing. Not at all. She most certainly would not allow herself to do anything so foolish.

So she waited, pretending to be up in her room reading but really just trying not to think about him getting ready, forcing herself not to go say goodbye. Only when he was out the door did she allow herself a quick peek out the window. He was dressed in black and white, his broad back impressive as he walked toward his car.

Most of the functions he had been invited to were informal due to the nature of the resort atmosphere of this area, but this party had been black tie. His suit was immaculate. He looked good in black. Even the starkness of the material couldn't hide the fact that he was muscled and fit.

"The women are going to love you, Donovan Barrett," Anna whispered.

And then, cursing herself for even thinking such a thought, Anna marched downstairs, picked up her list of things to do and started working again. Employee or not, she was not going to allow a man to dictate how she spent her free time.

Not even a man who was her boss.

Not even a man with eyes that made her consider things that could never be.

Or a man whose pain made her ache to help him, when she knew that she was the last person on earth who could do that.

"I'm not going to think of you at all tonight, Mr. Barrett," she muttered to herself as she scrubbed a spot on the wall for the third time.

* * *

The Williams mansion was aglow with what looked to be a thousand lights. Donovan parked his car and strolled up to the door, bracing himself for the night ahead.

He nodded to the black-clad servant who opened the door and led him to the back of the house where the sounds of chatter and clinking glasses could be heard.

As he entered the huge room filled with men in stark black and white, and women with perfect hair, perfectly made up faces and teeth so straight and immaculately white that it appeared as if a dentist magician had been at work here, Donovan relaxed slightly.

This was a world he knew, one he had inhabited in what already seemed like another lifetime.

He accepted a glass of champagne from a white-uniformed servant and moved toward the mass of guests.

A woman dressed in pale peach with auburn hair separated herself from the masses and moved toward him, holding out her hand. She looked at him appreciatively. It was a look he recognized. "You must be Donovan."

He tilted his head in acquiescence. "Are you Kendra Williams?" Although there was no real question of who she was. Besides the obvious fact that she was the one greeting him, there was the fact that Anna had told him that his hostess was a petite, dark-haired, beautiful green-eyed woman. Heir to this house, Mannion Way, and all of her family's fortune, she had been divorced for three years.

The woman tilted her head in a queenlike manner. "Yes, I'm Kendra, and I must say that getting a magnificent man like you here was a coup. Absolutely everyone wants you. Thank you for choosing me first."

The room behind her had gone amazingly silent, so this comment was heard by all. The silence didn't surprise Donovan. He was a stranger, a new toy. The old toys needed to know if he would fit in.

He laughed. "Well, I've taken some time to acclimate, but I'm enjoying the opportunity to finally meet my neighbors. Thank you for inviting me. Great old house. Superb wine. Wonderful company." Which said absolutely nothing but did the trick. The other potential hosts and hostesses had not been slighted but Kendra had not been put in her place, either.

The evening began in earnest, a steady din of meaningless chat and drinks and food that could drown out more serious thought.

It was what he had come for, Donovan thought. He would fit in here and pass the time. He smiled at those who smiled at him, ignoring the speculative glances of the women, married and otherwise, who were giving him obvious come-to-my-bedroom-later glances. When the conversation threatened to get personal he sidestepped and steered it back into more mundane topics about local tourism, the stock market and real estate.

He'd been raised to this kind of talk. He could rattle off such conversations in his sleep and it almost seemed as if that was just what he was doing. His mind began to go numb after a few minutes, but then that was a good thing. It was what he wanted. If, when a woman named Olivia Simms engaged him in a conversation about pier parties, he kept noting that her hands looked as if they had never been used for work, that was a glitch. If that thought was followed by a vision of Anna's pretty but useful hands, sending heat spiraling through him, it was a mistake, and an unkind one at that. Olivia was who and what she was, and he was of the same cloth. He shifted away from such thoughts.

Only once did he falter. To his right, he heard a small male exclamation, a female shriek and the crunching of glass beneath something heavy.

He turned to see Kendra, her dark eyebrows drawn together, her face a mask of fury, reprimanding a male servant who appeared to have dropped a glass, sloshing wine on a female guest. The woman was demanding reparation and the flustered servant was apologizing profusely.

Kendra's voice was low, but Donovan had excellent hearing, so he didn't miss her swift dismissal of the man despite his attempts to offer to pay for the guest's dry cleaning.

Other guests turned to look, then turned back to their conversations as if this wasn't an unusual occurrence.

The woman Donovan was talking to sighed. "Poor man," she said. "That dress was a Versace. He could never afford what it would cost to replace it." She took a sip of her own drink and placed her hand on Donovan's arm. "Now what were we discussing?"

"Something riveting, I'm sure," Donovan assured her as he made an effort to bring a smooth, controlled end to the conversation. Less than two minutes later he smiled at her. "Please accept my apologies, but I'm afraid I have to leave. I have an early appointment."

"So suddenly? It must be important," she said with a raised eyebrow.

"It is," he admitted, but he didn't want to think what that appointment was going to be. Recounting the evening to Anna?

No, he wouldn't do that. But he really did have to go. The memory of Kendra firing her servant nagged at him. Anger was churning in his gut. Smiling was no longer an option.

He excused himself to Kendra, saying all the right and polite things, bid the other guests goodbye, then hurried out the door.

Breathing in the clean fresh air, he tried to clear his mind, hoping for luck. He fought against analyzing what he planned to do next.

Sprinting beyond the area where the guests' cars were parked, Donovan found a few older and considerably less sleek automobiles. He hoped his guess was right and that he had timed things properly and would find the person he was seeking. If he missed his chance, he would have to do detective work, and his most likely source of information was Anna. He didn't want to talk to her about this.

Glancing around, Donovan made a quick visual inspection of the area. There were only a few dim lights out here. The sky was clouded and moonless. Visibility was limited.

No luck.

He waited for his vision to adjust to the darkness, listening for the sound of a car door or an engine. Finally, he began to make out shapes more clearly and this time he saw what he had missed. A man sat on a rock next to a rather battered pickup truck. His head was in his hands.

Donovan approached him.

The man looked up, wary.

"I just came from the party," Donovan said, gesturing toward the house.

The man faltered, looked scared. "I didn't mean to make such a stupid mistake. I looked away just for a minute and...well, it was clumsiness, pure and simple."

Donovan ignored him. "I'm looking for help at my house. Can you use some work?"

The man's eyes lit up, but he didn't jump. "Doing what?"

Donovan almost smiled. "Nothing illegal," he promised, although he didn't have a clue what he was hiring the man for. He already had a gardener. "Do you know anything about plumbing?"

The man looked despondent. "Not really."

"Electrical work?"

"Only a little bit."

Donovan frowned. "Can you lift things?"

The man smiled. "Sure. I'm strong."

"Good. Show up at Morning View Manor the day after tomorrow at 9:00 a.m. sharp."

"What will I be doing?"

"Grunt work. Greeting guests. Assisting my housekeeper. A little bit of everything." Donovan made it up as he went along.

"All right, yes. Thank you, Mr...."

"Barrett. And there's no need to thank me. Just do a good job."

The man nodded. Donovan wanted to stipulate one more thing. *Don't tell Anna how I hired you. She already thinks I'm better than I really am or ever was.* But that would have been too bizarre, even more bizarre than the fact that he had rushed after the man to offer him work.

What was that about?

But Donovan knew. When Kendra had been firing the man, Donovan had only been able to think about how he would have felt if it had been Anna who had been called on the carpet for spilling a drink on a guest's dress. And there was something about Anna that made him want to be a better man.

"You're an idiot, Barrett," he told himself as he headed home.

That was all right. He could deal with being an idiot. He just couldn't deal with guilt. His life had been filled with guilt these past few years, and Anna made him feel even more guilty.

He had the awful feeling that he was going to somehow hurt her, and that there was nothing he could do to stop that.

What a ridiculous thought. He was Anna's boss, nothing more. Nor would he ever be more. Thank goodness.

CHAPTER SIX

ANNA woke that morning, groggy. She had done just what she'd planned to do the night before, finished her work and then gone to bed.

Yet she had been perfectly aware that Donovan had returned home at two in the morning. The party must have been a hit.

That was good. It made it that much easier to remind herself that Donovan was her boss, a man born to mingle with the rich and famous. Now she could get back to her life and think only of her child, her dream.

At least, those were her thoughts in the middle of the night. But in the morning her head ached and she was glad that this was her day off. Still, she took the time to tell Linette, the cook, to make something that would keep since Donovan would most likely be late to breakfast.

Anna prepared to plan her day, fighting the headache that had resulted from her lack of sleep. It was obvious that the day wasn't going to be one of her finest. And that was before the phone rang, its piercing and insistent din sending her flying to answer it.

"Barrett residence."

"Anna, it's me," her friend Bridget said. Bridget worked in one of the gift shops in town. "Did you hear what went on last night? Did your Mr. Barrett tell you?"

The possibilities immediately ran through Anna's head. Visions of Donovan with a beautiful woman, with several women draped over his arms or pressing up against his chest came to mind. The possibility that he might have slept with one of them presented itself.

Anna closed her eyes and ran a hand over her forehead. "I haven't seen him yet."

"Good. I get to do the honors then," Bridget said as she launched into a tale of how Kendra Williams had fired John Jessup on the spot at the party last night and then Donovan had hired him.

"What do you think that's about?" Bridget asked.

Anna tried not to feel relief. Her mind was suddenly a tornado of speculation, but as good a friend as Bridget was, Anna wasn't going to gossip about Donovan with her. "Donovan probably just needed some help, and John was there."

"But he ruined Meredith Talbott's dress. She's probably spitting mad at him."

"That probably won't matter. John won't be interacting with any guests. Donovan doesn't entertain."

Bridget snorted. "He will. Wait and see. Now that they've seen him, the women will be rushing your house. I've already heard one or two in here whispering about his broad shoulders. They'll want to see what else he has to offer. Like property. Sooner or later, he'll have to open the doors of Morning View and let them in."

And she would be the one serving the drinks this time, Anna knew, while the local heiresses and wealthy divorcées did their best to entice her boss to their beds.

"Then I'd better make sure the house is in top shape," she told her friend just before she hung up the phone. After all, who was she to criticize the women of the town for wanting Donovan? He was an attractive and intelligent man.

"And a kind man," she reminded herself, thinking of how he had hired John.

What's more, just because Donovan had said that he didn't want to marry didn't mean that he might not change his mind. Lots of the women he was meeting now would be willing to give up motherhood to have him. Maybe he could be happy again.

Despite the fact that something dark and unacceptable ran through her at the thought of him marrying, she stopped herself cold. Because she did hope that he could be happy again. She wondered how he felt about last night.

But of course, she couldn't ask.

Donovan braced his feet on the floor, lay back and lifted the weighted bar, pressing upward slowly, exhaling, then inhaling as he lowered the bar to his chest. His muscles tightened, his body strained as he tried to push himself harder and concentrate only on what he was doing.

A short time later he sat up, admitting that while the exercise might be good for his body it wasn't doing anything to quell his restlessness. Furthermore, the incidents of the last evening had left a bad taste in his mouth. He needed fresh air.

After taking a quick shower and dressing, Donovan fully intended to head for the lake. He might even take a walk partway down the shore path. For half a second he thought of the family Anna had driven home, the little boy. Then, shaking his head, he headed toward the door.

A feminine giggle stopped him cold.

An unknown feminine giggle. It wasn't Anna's. He knew Anna's voice. Sometimes he dreamed Anna's voice.

Donovan turned. A woman several years Anna's senior was standing on the stairs looking down at him.

Almost immediately Anna appeared, a frown on her face. "I'm sorry, Donovan. Some friends have dropped by. We didn't mean to disturb you."

"You didn't. And…"

She waited.

He shrugged. "It's your day off. You should feel free to have your friends over."

"Oh, I like him," the other woman said. "The John Jessup thing wasn't just a fluke."

Donovan frowned, not understanding.

"The man you hired last night," Anna explained. "Didn't he tell you his name?"

Donovan smiled sheepishly. "I didn't ask."

A look of concern came over Anna's face. "You didn't even ask? You hired him without knowing anything about him?"

"I knew he needed a job."

And he had known something else. He'd known that he wouldn't have wanted Anna to face the humiliation of being fired because she had made a simple mistake.

Right now she was looking at him with soft eyes. "Did you eat breakfast?"

"Not yet."

"Oh, good," the other woman said. "We have food. Anna always feeds us when we come over. Maybe you'd like to join us."

Anna was looking horrified. "Nan, he's got better things to do with his time than eat with us."

"No, I don't." The words surprised even him.

"Well, then," Nan said. "Anna?"

Donovan waited. He should let her off the hook, claim to have other plans. Yet he didn't. He tried not to wonder why.

Anna stared at Donovan and bit her lip. Already the day was getting away from her. Nan and Paula had both shown up unannounced, probably driven here by Bridget's tales. She adored both of them. Together with Bridget, they had saved her sanity when her sanity had needed saving, and they never questioned her baby plans even though she knew they wanted to. But there was no question in her mind that they were here to check out Donovan.

She didn't want anyone trying to decide if he was good or bad. Hadn't he gone through enough?

"I'm not sure this is a good idea," she said.

"Of course," he said, studying her intently. "It's your day off. These are your friends."

And he was her boss, she reminded herself.

"I'm not worried that you're going to fire me because of anything that goes on today. It's not that you're intruding. It's just…"

She paused, flustered, her hands gesturing as she tried to find the right words.

He grinned. "It's okay, Anna. I'm gone." He turned to head back into the other part of the house.

"Don't pay any attention to Anna, Mr. Barrett. I know what the problem is. Anna's just afraid we'll interrogate you," Nan said with a laugh.

Donovan turned and raised a brow, studying Anna.

She squirmed and gave Nan a dirty look. "Nan's a sweetheart but she's right. She and Paula will ask you all kinds of questions. You're a bit of a celebrity, especially after the John Jessup thing."

He swore. "I didn't want you to know about that."

Anna stopped fidgeting. "Why not?"

"Because it makes me look like I was doing something noble. I wasn't. It was an impulse, a knee-jerk reaction."

"Which won't win you any points with Kendra Williams, either," Nan offered.

Anna gave her a warning look.

But Donovan laughed. "You might be right, but that's okay. I didn't come to Lake Geneva to earn points with anyone. Opinions don't matter to me. And I'm not looking for a woman or a relationship, so that's not a problem."

Nan looked a bit surprised. "You're not even interested in the women who'd like to get you in bed?"

"Nan!" Anna's voice actually squeaked.

"Well they are," her friend said. "People are talking."

Anna scowled at Nan. "*We're* not talking."

She felt Donovan's light touch on the small of her back. "It's all right, Anna. Newcomers are fair game for gossip. It's to be expected. And no, Nan, I'm not in the market for a woman of any variety right now."

Nan shook her head and shrugged. "You are definitely not a typical man, Mr. Barrett."

Anna smiled at her friend's look of disbelief. Nan was a large, curvy and very earthy woman. She liked her pleasures and thought everyone else should feel the same. Anna was a constant trial to her.

"Come have lunch," Anna told Donovan. Now that he had made his complete indifference to her as a woman clear and she had shown no concern about his indifference, Nan and Paula wouldn't worry and they would most likely behave themselves. Besides, she knew that if Donovan left he would end up kicking around the house avoiding his demons. Nan and Paula weren't exactly angels, but they weren't demons most of the time, either. They just watched their friends' backs, as she did.

Anna wondered who watched Donovan's back, but then she already knew the answer to that, didn't she? No one did.

Glancing at him, she realized that she must have been silent too long. Donovan was giving her that speculative, I-can-see-through-you look that always made her too self-conscious. She would just bet that his former patients couldn't hide anything from him. Remembering his reaction to the little boy on the shore path and his reaction to John Jessup, she had no doubt that he had been a wonderful, caring doctor.

But he didn't want that anymore. And he was waiting for her to take the lead now. He wouldn't appreciate her delving into his business.

"This way," she said softly and nodded toward the stairs just as if this wasn't his house and he didn't know where she stayed.

They all turned toward Anna's room. Nan led the way and Donovan brought up the rear.

Anna tried not to feel self-conscious; it was all but impossible. She was wearing her usual faded jeans, and they fit a bit snugly over her butt. The realization that Donovan couldn't help but end up staring at that part of her anatomy whether he wanted to or not made her heart start to do terribly acrobatic things she wasn't used to. She wanted to rush up the stairs and end the sensation, but she resisted the urge, trying not to let her hips sway. He already had Dana Wellinton swinging her belly in his face. She didn't want him to think she was trying to get his attention, too.

When she got to the top of the stairs, she turned to the left where her room was located. Like all the rooms at Morning View, it was large and airy. She had, of course, left the basics of the room alone, but she had tried to make it her own.

The room was done in jade and white, and she had set out touches of sunflower gold here and there. There was a vase she'd gotten at a garage sale, a thrift shop scarf she'd draped halfway across the mirror. The room had always looked cozy to her in the past, but today, despite the table she and Paula and Nan had dragged in for their lunch, the bed seemed enormous.

Anna did her best to ignore it.

"You need a bigger room," Donovan said.

She turned and saw that he was staring at the bed, too.

Nan laughed, and Paula, who was crossing the room to meet them, joined in.

"I love this room," Anna insisted as she hurriedly introduced Paula to Donovan.

"I have others," he argued.

"I'm well aware of every room in the house," she answered, a bit haughtily.

Donovan's lips turned up slightly. "Of course. You're the housekeeper."

Paula hooted at that. "Anna, I can't believe you're playing housekeeper. She was always the poet in school," she explained to Donovan.

He raised a brow. "A poet. And I have you washing windows?"

Anna frowned at Paula and raised her chin when she turned back to Donovan. "I happen to love washing windows."

He grinned at that. "Well then, I'm happy to be providing you with an activity you love."

For half a second, Anna thought about Dana and Kendra and half a dozen other socialites who would adore doing something they loved with Donovan. That

activity certainly wouldn't be washing windows. Heat
filled her and she did her best to tamp it down.

"Thank you," she told Donovan. "You know I appreciate the work."

And that was all there was to say. He knew. She had
all but begged for this job. So, Anna trotted off to get
an extra chair. When Donovan started to get up to help
her, she gave him a quelling look.

"It's my day off. I get to call the shots."

Apparently the man didn't hear well. He followed her
and was there beside her when she found an armchair
and started to wrestle it down the hall. Immediately he
took hold of the chair, stopping her momentum and
bracing the weight against his body. "I'm the guest
today, and I was taught that a hostess didn't tell a guest
no. That's heavy. Give it to me."

Anna started to argue, but only the width of the chair
was between them. His large hand was braced near her
own slender one. The comparison made her feel
feminine, a sensation she wasn't used to. His nearness
made it difficult to breathe…or think…or know where
to look without looking into his eyes or staring at his
mouth. And arguing would prolong the discomfiting
proximity. At least that was what she told herself.

In the end, she let him take the chair from her and
walked beside him. Was this how it had been with his
wife? she wondered and then was immediately appalled.

As soon as she was able, she slipped away to the
kitchen to get their lunch.

"Oh, Linette is a dream," Paula was declaring as

Anna came in with the food. "You certainly know how to hire the best," she told Donovan.

"Anna," was all he said, and Nan nodded.

"Anna knows who's the best at everything around here," she agreed.

Donovan's eyes turned brighter. "You should give tours."

"I have," Anna admitted.

"Sounds enjoyable."

"Yes, but this pays better."

She immediately regretted her comment, because she knew what would follow. She looked at her friends, but it was too late.

"Anna really wants a baby, and no one works harder than she does to achieve her goals," Paula said.

Immediately a silence fell into the room. Anna knew that Donovan had been caught off guard. His eyes turned suddenly dark.

"Paula," Anna said softly, but Donovan was already squaring those broad shoulders and turning toward Paula and Nan.

"And how about you? Are you like Anna? Have you lived in Lake Geneva all your life?"

"All," Nan agreed.

"Most of it," Paula countered. She looked a bit uncomfortable and when Anna looked at her, she mouthed an "I'm sorry."

Anna nodded, but Donovan had gone on to his next question, asking Nan and Paula about their favorite places in the area. By the time the two of them got ready to leave, they had scribbled down a list of "must sees" for Donovan and pressed the pieces of paper into his hands.

"He's gorgeous," Nan said as Anna saw her out the door.

"He's charming," Paula agreed.

"Be careful," they said together.

"I thought you liked him," Anna said, wide-eyed.

"We do," Nan said. "That's the problem. What woman wouldn't like him? And you're sharing the same space with him. When he takes a shower don't you just…imagine him?"

"Oh, yes," Paula agreed. "That man is hot. How could you not imagine him naked?"

Anna suddenly felt a bit faint. She had tried her best *not* to think of Donovan that way. "Donovan is my employer," she emphasized. "I clean his house. I wash his walls. He's appeared in the society pages. He goes to parties at the local mansions."

She stared at her friends.

"You're right," Nan said. "He makes it easy to forget that he's got money and connections and that he gets invited to the best parties."

She could almost forget, Anna thought when her friends had gone, if his upcoming evenings and days weren't booked with events at the houses of people she would never socialize with in her lifetime.

When she turned to go back upstairs, Donovan was waiting at the bottom, his arms crossed as he leaned on the wall in a casual pose.

Anna took a deep breath.

"Your friends are very nice," he told her.

She nodded.

"They're worried about you," he added.

Her gaze grew wary. "Sometimes they worry, but they forget I can take care of myself."

"Nan told me to be nice to you."

"What? When?" Anna frowned, her mouth open.

"When you went to get the food."

"I'm sorry. They've both known me a long time, and they're some of my closest friends, but they had no right to say something like that."

He shook his head. "They did. They know how much you want a child. They know that we spend our nights alone in this house."

"Mr. Barrett," she stammered.

"Donovan," he said. "We've moved beyond formalities. Call me Donovan."

Anna swallowed nervously. "Donovan, don't worry. I would never even consider that you would think of me that way. I—"

He pushed off the wall and stepped close to her. Pushing one finger beneath her chin, he bent and touched his lips to hers.

Her eyes fluttered shut. Her breath caught. She fought not to react, but his lips were so warm, his touch so compelling, she couldn't help tipping her head and kissing him back.

"Let's have honesty between us," he said. "I do desire you and I have from the beginning, wrong though that may be."

If she were totally honest she would say that she desired him, too, but that would leave her too vulnerable. She'd been that before, and she couldn't do it again.

"Don't," she said.

He let her go. "I won't. I just wanted you to be aware that your friends were right to be concerned. There's something about you…something vibrant. You're an incredibly desirable woman, Anna. I should hire someone else to be here at night."

"That would be foolish. I trust you. And what would you tell the person they were being hired for?"

He smiled at that. "You're right. There's no need. I would never hurt you, and touching you would hurt you."

She knew why. Because there could be no future between someone like him and someone like her.

"I shouldn't have invited you to lunch with me and my friends. We're not the same."

He shook his head. "I liked them. They say what they mean. They wouldn't let me get away with anything."

"You're right about that," she said with a laugh. "Paula and Nan are direct."

"And you?" he asked.

She stared up into his eyes. "I'm direct, too. You're an amazingly attractive man, and I've wanted to know what kissing you would be like."

His eyes darkened. His gaze honed in on her lips. "What was it like?"

Anna tried to keep breathing normally. She touched her lips. "It was something I enjoyed far too much."

Donovan groaned.

She held up a hand. "But not only do you and I come from different social classes, we want different things. We could never meet halfway and I wouldn't do anything to risk my job here." She didn't repeat her desire to have a baby, but she didn't have to.

"You want a man who'll give you a child," he agreed.

"I *need* a child, not a man," she said.

Donovan brushed his knuckles across her cheek. "Be careful what you wish for, Anna," he said. "I don't want you to get hurt."

"I'm very careful," she said, even though she wished she could be more careful with him.

He smiled then, faintly, and stepped away. "Go enjoy the rest of your day off. Maybe you should take an extra day off, too, since so much of this one is gone."

"Thank you, but I'll be back at work tomorrow."

He turned to go and she noticed the pieces of paper sticking out of his pocket. Nan and Paula's suggestions for things to do in Lake Geneva.

Anna held out her hand. "I'll recycle those."

He put his hand over his pocket. "No, I might try some of these. Maybe even today."

Alone, she thought. He spent so much time alone, except…

"You have another party later today," she reminded him.

He grimaced. "Yes, I remember. Would you like to go with me?"

She froze. Surely he was joking. He'd already offended a few people by hiring John after everyone had seen Kendra fire him. What would happen if he turned up at an affair with his housekeeper?

Probably nothing. The women would still fall all over him. It would be Anna who would feel completely uncomfortable.

"Thank you, but I can't," she said.

It seemed "I can't" were two words she uttered a lot. I can't find a good man. I can't have a baby. I can't spend any more time alone with Donovan Barrett.

And she wouldn't, either. No more tea parties. No more responding to his touch. From now on she would be completely professional in every way.

CHAPTER SEVEN

WHY had he done that? Donovan was still asking himself the next day as he listened to Anna's footsteps in the hallway, watched her endangering herself by climbing on ladders to dust the tops of bookshelves and heard her singing a recent rock song as she tackled the grout in the bathroom.

He'd kissed her, and he could still feel the imprint of her warm lips on his own. His fingers itched to slide over her skin again, to gather her close.

"Insanity," he muttered. He had gone to another party last night, an informal picnic on the grass with torches lighting the night and all the women wearing slinky sundresses.

They weren't all like Dana and Kendra. In fact, most of the guests were fine people with intelligent minds. They obviously had come to this area because they loved the beauty of the scenery. One woman in particular had thanked him for hiring John the other day.

"The rest of us were too shocked to say anything," she said. "We didn't want to embarrass him further.

We're all well aware that the town of Lake Geneva would cease to function without the people who work in the shops and restaurants and who clean our houses and keep our gardens and make the town hum. We'd be lost without them. Most of us wouldn't have successful businesses without their patronage, and they deserve our respect and fair working conditions as well as a decent wage, but we weren't thinking about that the other night. You, on the other hand, actually did something about the situation. You offered John work and repaired his damaged ego."

"I just reacted," Donovan had told her. And if he'd been thinking at all that night, he had been thinking about Anna more so than John, but he couldn't say that here. It would be unkind to her. It would bring her attention she didn't want.

He'd continued his conversation with the woman who had been very beautiful with a lush body and gorgeous blond hair. But all night he kept thinking of serious gray eyes and a voice telling him that she needed a child, not a man. He remembered her walking down to the shore path to meet the man with the little boy…

The doorbell cut into Donovan's thoughts. It rang once, twice, three times.

Anna was running the vacuum cleaner.

He started toward the door. The whirring of the vacuum stopped as the doorbell rang for the fourth time.

Donovan reached the hallway just as Anna swung the door open.

A boy stood on the threshold.

"Frank," she said, and though Donovan couldn't see Anna's face he could hear the smile in her voice. "Is it that time already?"

"First of the month. Time to do your part to keep the news coming," he joked with a big grin on his face.

Donovan fought to keep breathing. The boy was about twelve with flyaway longish brown hair, green eyes and an infectious smile. He waited politely for Anna's response.

"Well, we definitely don't want the news to stop coming," she agreed. "Wait right here and I'll be back."

She turned and noticed Donovan standing there and the smile on her face froze.

"I—this is Frank," she said, her voice sounding a bit weak. "Frank delivers the newspaper."

Frank smiled more broadly. "Are you Mr. Barrett?"

Donovan struggled to fight the tightness in his chest. He fought not to think about the fact that Ben might have been much like this boy one day had he lived.

"Yes," was all Donovan could manage.

"My mom told me that if I should ever see you I should tell you that she hopes you're enjoying Lake Geneva."

"That's very nice of her, and…yes, I am, thank you," Donovan said.

The boy chuckled and the sound of it shot right through Donovan's soul. "Hey, don't thank me. I'd never have thought to ask you somethin' like that. Maybe I'd ask how fast your Jaguar can go. Have to obey Mom, though. She hears everything, and if she found out I'd met you and hadn't remembered to ask…well…"

"She wouldn't hit you?" Donovan asked.

The boys eyes grew wide with shock. "Mom? Hit me?" He laughed. "No, she'd just put on her disappointed face, probably give me a lecture about my manners. I'd end up feeling like a jerk." He blew out a breath. "I hate feeling like that, so if you meet her, could you tell her that I remembered to ask?"

Donovan couldn't keep from smiling even though the pain in his chest grew worse. What a great kid and how hard it was to keep breathing and smiling and just standing here when Ben's memory and thoughts of all that Ben might have turned out to be were assaulting him. He managed a nod. "I'll tell her your manners were great."

Donovan's voice wasn't as steady as he would have liked. He felt Anna's touch on his sleeve. Her eyes were dark with concern. Somewhere in there when he and Frank had been talking she had gone and got some money to pay the boy. She handed Frank a check along with a tip.

"Thanks, Anna. You're the best. You never make me come back later."

"I wouldn't do that, Frank. You're very dependable at your job," she said.

The boy practically glowed. "Hey, if you see Mom…"

"I'll repeat the compliment," she promised with a smile.

The boy said his goodbyes, then turned and loped out to the end of the walk where his bike was waiting. "Nice meeting you, Mr. Barrett. See you, Anna." He waved, and so, of course, Donovan waved back.

But as soon as the boy was out of sight, Donovan turned to go. He needed to be alone, to shut his eyes, to block out the memories and the ache of lost hopes.

"Donovan," Anna said, and he felt her arm on his sleeve again.

He looked down at her. "Don't worry. It's fine," he said. "I can't go through my whole life never meeting boys who will remind me that my own son died before he reached that age."

"But this time was unnecessary. I should have thought about the fact that Frank was coming by today and either met him at the street or at the very least warned you ahead of time so you could prepare yourself."

As if he could ever do that. She must have been thinking the same thing because her eyes looked suddenly anguished. "Next month Frank and I will make other arrangements. I can mail the bill. It's what most people do. I just—"

He knew what her hesitation was for. She didn't pay the bill by mail because she liked Frank and it was a chance to talk to him.

"He's a great kid," Donovan said.

"Yes, he is."

"Glad I met him," he said, and he was glad in a way. But he was also sorry as well. "I have a few things to do," he told her and he started to walk away, but…he knew she was worried. Donovan didn't want that. And he didn't want her to feel guilty in the least.

He turned back.

"Anna, I hope you have a child just as nice as Frank

someday. Hell, what am I saying? You will. Any kid you raise will turn out well." Somewhere he found a smile.

Somewhere she found one, too, although it was a sad one. Her lips…he wanted to touch her lips and turn her smile into one of gladness, but that would be unfair. He could never give her what she needed.

Donovan let her go, but hours later he was still thinking of Anna's sad smile. He realized that for the first time in a long time, he had encountered a child and ended up spending the next few hours thinking about something other than Ben.

He listened for Anna and heard her humming to herself as she worked. She said she loved being a house-keeper. He knew she was loyal to her friends and inspired loyalty in others. Plus, she had brought homey touches to this huge building and was obviously well-liked by Frank, who was of an age when boys often didn't want anything to do with adults.

In other words, Anna was perfect mother material. She longed for a child with all her heart, just as much as he shied away from the thought of ever having another.

Surely at least one of the two of them should have what they wanted. Maybe it was time to stop avoiding painful topics and ask a few important questions.

Anna was setting the table for Donovan that evening, trying once again to make a single table setting look somehow interesting rather than lonely. She moved the salt shaker out a bit farther, replaced the tall vase of flowers with a long low one that was less overwhelming. She was considering the effect and thinking about adding a couple of candles when the sound of footsteps made her look up.

"It's occurred to me that I've been an insensitive male who probably doesn't appreciate your efforts nearly enough," Donovan said, standing in the doorway, the light filtering in behind him.

She shrugged. "People enjoy a meal more when the table looks better even if they don't think about it. This one seems a bit sparse."

"No problem. I can fix that." He went to the china cabinet, pulled out another place setting and arranged it on the table. "Have dinner with me."

Anna's eyes widened. She took a deep breath. Had he thought she was angling for something like this?

"No, I'm fine. I just—"

"Anna, sit," Donovan ordered. He was frowning, his eyebrows dark slashes.

She sat. But she wasn't happy.

"I won't bite," he promised.

"I know that."

"And I won't kiss you again."

She squirmed on her chair. "I know that, too." But now that he'd mentioned it, her lips—and his lips— were all she could think of.

"You're not supposed to eat dinner with your house-keeper," she said suddenly, trying to get her mind off kisses and back on the topic at hand.

"Ah, I see. Rules." He smiled.

She managed to glare even though her heart wasn't really in it. "Rules have a purpose."

"Do you always play by the rules, then?"

Anna thought back to how she had all but forced him to hire her for this job, and immediately dropped her pretend glare. "You know I don't."

"Don't look so sad, Anna. You haven't broken any laws."

"I know. Why?" she asked.

"Why?"

"Why did you ask me to eat dinner with you?"

He leaned back in his chair and blew out a breath. "I have something I want to discuss with you."

"A job evaluation? Or…maybe there's some problem. Or…something you need me to do. Or…"

He held up one hand. "Nothing bad. Nothing that should concern you. Let's just have dinner and then we'll talk."

It was a reasonable suggestion, but waiting made eating difficult. Anna had never been good at waiting.

"Does this have to do with the parties you've been going to? Your social situation? Maybe something that happened at lunch with the girls yesterday? Another employee? Do you need me to talk to Linette or John or even Clyde?"

Donovan put down his fork. His lips lifted slightly. "Let's go sit on the deck," he suggested. "I just have some questions. Not bad questions and nothing that would require you to admonish another employee. I don't have any problems with the staff."

Taking a deep breath, Anna studied his expression. Maybe this had to do with one of the women he had met recently. Bridget had told her a woman at the shop yesterday wanted Anna to ask some questions about Donovan's likes and dislikes. He was obviously fresh meat and the interested women were looking for artillery. Maybe, in spite of his assertions that he wasn't interested in getting involved, he'd met someone he liked. He was a normal man, after all. At least, he certainly kissed like one.

No, that was wrong. He kissed like no man she'd ever kissed before. He'd made her flare and burn and melt like a birthday candle.

Anna cleared her throat and forced herself to rise and stop—please, stop—thinking about Donovan's physical talents. "Fresh air would be nice," she agreed, and followed him out onto the deck.

A breeze blew off the lake and lifted strands of her hair, brushing them against her cheeks. She turned to Donovan, waiting.

"You were good with Frank today," he said.

She ducked her head, wondering where this was leading. "He's easy to talk to."

"I'll bet you were good with that little boy the other day, too."

"Why are you saying these things, Donovan?" Her voice came out shaky and scared. At least that was how it seemed to her.

"You want a child. You want to adopt. Why?"

The question was like a lightning bolt slashing through the air on a sunny day. It caught her by surprise.

"Why do you ask?"

"I'm just wondering how important it is to you, what your rationale is. It's prying, I know."

She took a deep breath and shook her head. "I'm not fond of discussing my past, but it's not a secret. My friends and plenty of my acquaintances know, and since I twisted your arm to get this job, you deserve to know something of my motives, too. I didn't have a glowing childhood. My father deserted us. My mother…wasn't kind or loving. Fortunately, other people were. Neighbors. Friends. But they all belonged to other people, really. They weren't mine in the way a parent should be." She looked at him to see if he understood.

His expression was unreadable. She suspected this subject was hurting him, but he wasn't backing away. "Your parents weren't there for you. I'm familiar with that kind of nonexistent parenting. I was a workaholic and seldom available for my family."

An ache went through her. "It's not the same. You cared about them. My father didn't care at all. My mother resented the fact that she had to raise me, so much so that she once told me she hated me."

Anger flashed in Donovan's eyes. "That's criminal."

She shrugged. "It's the way things were. I survived."

Donovan shook his head.

Anna raised her chin. "What?"

"You amaze me, Anna. It takes a strong and special person to get past something like that and not turn out bitter."

"I'm not a saint or an angel. I *am* bitter, but as I said, I was lucky enough to have other parent figures."

"And now you want to raise a child to attempt to stamp out the past?"

"No, not at all. The past is what it is. It's gone, done. But there are children out there who need love, and I know better than many the importance of love to a child. I can give that. I *want* to give that kind of unconditional love." She struggled to keep her voice steady.

Looking up, she saw that Donovan was studying her. He put down his glass and stepped closer, taking her hand.

"More prying," he said. "May I ask…what steps you've taken to achieve your goal?"

She took a deep breath, tried not to think about how his hand felt, curved around hers. His fingers were long, his skin was warm. She felt protected. She felt that what she had to say mattered.

"I've done research online, at the library and by talking to adoption agencies."

"But you haven't taken the next step."

"No. I'm not going to do this halfway. I want my child to feel secure, and that includes feeling financially secure. I'm saving every penny I can. I have to know that if I got sick for a while, I'd still have enough to cover our expenses. And…I don't want to take a chance of the agency thinking that I might be a bad risk."

He lifted her hand, turning it so that her work-roughened palm was visible. For one breathless second she thought he was going to press his lips to her skin.

Instead he looked directly into her eyes. "I can't see anyone thinking of you as a risk. You're obviously dedicated and driven and giving."

She laughed. "You only think that because I was so pushy about getting this job."

He laughed, too, and she felt the sound echoing through her fingers as he brushed his thumb across her palm, his skin sliding against hers. Heat spread outward from where they touched, radiating throughout her body.

As if Donovan felt it, too, he released her suddenly. "All right, I've interrogated you enough. I should let you go."

Automatically she turned. She was, after all, an employee and she had been dismissed, but one thing kept her from leaving.

"It wasn't just idle curiosity, was it?" She looked back over her shoulder.

He pressed his lips together, then shook his head. "No. It wasn't. A child is such a big responsibility. They feel so deeply. They need so much. I just needed to know how much you wanted this."

She bit her lip. "You were worried that a child might be shortchanged."

"Another child," he corrected. "I shortchanged my child, and I can never go back and fix that. Ever. As you said, the past is gone." His words were low. His voice was tight.

Somehow Anna blinked and held back any response to what he'd said and what he was obviously feeling. He was flailing himself, and there was nothing she could say that wouldn't sound trite or pathetic or wrong. So she gave a tight nod. "I understand. That makes sense." Again she started to leave.

But he touched her, ever so lightly on her shoulder. Sensation slipped through her.

"I was wrong," he said. "I was wrong to question your motives. I already know that you're the right kind of woman for motherhood."

She turned back to him then and touched his sleeve. What she wanted to say was that he was the right kind of man for fatherhood, too. She was sure that she was right, and yet…she was also wrong. He had once been the right kind of man for fatherhood. It was evident in everything he said, all that he did and the way he treated people. But he had left fatherhood behind. He didn't want it anymore, and she couldn't blame him.

"Thank you," she whispered. "Very much," she added, a bit more primly.

He smiled then. "You're welcome. Very much so." And the smile traveled from his lips to his eyes. "But I wasn't fishing for gratitude. That's not what I want."

Donovan's smile relieved Anna's concern, but it didn't put an end to the tension sliding through her. She looked into that golden-brown gaze and instantly became aware that she was still touching him, linked to him. The heat of his body warmed her fingertips. She had a sudden and intense need to rest her palms against his chest. She remembered how his mouth had felt against her own and she wondered what it would be like to have his arms around her.

Her body jerked. She couldn't think straight. "What

were you fishing for? What *do* you want?" she asked, recalling his words. Her hand flew over her mouth. "I can't believe I said that."

He touched her cheek. His smile turned to a grin. "I can't, either. And no, I wasn't fishing for that, but I want it very much. You'd better go."

She stood there, still frozen.

"Anna. Now. Please. For your own good, go."

She fled and didn't stop until she was in her room. Once there, she dug out every magazine she owned. No books. She didn't have enough concentration for books. But turning the pages of the magazines, she saw black hair with a silver streak she wanted to touch. The too-pretty male models made her think of someone a bit more rugged, a man with eyes of golden-brown and fingers that…

Her heartbeat sped up. She flipped the page. A man held a woman in his arms, molding her body to his.

Anna let out a muffled cry, then threw down the magazine and lay down, pushing a pillow over her head.

Darn the man for being who and what he was. And as for herself, she was turning out to be every bit as bad as Dana Wellinton. Her heart's desire might be a child of her own, but right now her body wanted Donovan Barrett's touch.

Tonight was going to be long and tense, and tomorrow, when she would have to face him again…

"Don't think about tomorrow," she whispered to herself.

She did her best. She lay there, trying to get back to

normal. Then a part of her realized that she was half-buried beneath a stack of magazines with a pillow over her head. The situation would be laughable if it weren't so pathetic.

Slowly she sat up. She stacked the magazines and turned off the light. She took a deep energizing breath and forced her thoughts as far away from Donovan as she could.

"There. Almost better," she said, but she knew it was just a matter of seeing the man again, or heaven forbid, touching him again, and she would go back to being a mess. This had happened before. She'd started having feelings for a man and she'd lost. But those times she had at least thought she might win. She'd had justification for hope of a future.

With Donovan there could never be any future.

Anna groaned at her own stupidity. Wanting a man to kiss you when there could be no tomorrow was just asking to have your heart trashed.

She closed her eyes, filled her lungs, tried to think logically.

Work, she thought. I need work. Lots of it. Far, far away from my too wealthy, too handsome, too not-for-me boss.

She might be the housekeeper, but tomorrow she just might add a page to her duties and help Clyde do some weeding in the garden. Surely if she was away from the house she would be safe from this ridiculous ache she had for her boss.

CHAPTER EIGHT

DONOVAN stared out the window, trying to decide the right thing to do. Anna wanted a child, and every day children were born to mothers who either didn't want them or couldn't afford to raise them. But adoption was still a long and complicated procedure, especially for someone struggling to get through it on their own.

She'd said that she'd done her research and he believed her. Anna was a determined woman. When she wanted something she went after it.

"No question about that," he said to himself, remembering how she had rushed around the house from one task to the next trying to prove herself to him.

Anna was definitely dedicated to her dream of adoption, but she didn't have access to all the information that was available. She wouldn't be able to unearth all the private avenues there might be the way someone could who had access to primary sources.

Donovan ran one hand over his jaw. Some of those primary sources were doctors, ones he'd worked with, ones he'd been friends with. Those he'd left behind and hadn't thought ever to see or talk to again.

He was no longer a member of the medical community and he didn't want to be. He couldn't be.

But Anna wanted to adopt a child. And she was alone.

For several moments Donovan just sat there, staring at the ripples on the lake. Boats skimmed over the surface. Birds glided and dipped on the breeze. The pristine-white of piers connected the green of the lawns and trees to the blue of the water. The tranquility should have been soothing, and it would have been if not for the step he was poised to take.

You don't have to do this, he reminded himself. It's interfering. That's not your way.

But he remembered Anna's smile as she spoke to Frank, the softness of her voice, the rightness of it all. Some people weren't meant for parenthood, but some were.

He took a deep breath and plunged onward.

No matter her physical limitations, Anna was born to be a mother. It could happen. It should happen. If a constant source of money was all that was standing in the way…

He reached for the telephone. Money wasn't all. Adoption could be a painful, twisting maze, fraught with disappointment, frustration and setback. Information was what was needed.

Punching in the numbers that would connect him, he waited for the past to rush in.

Ben. His practice. His home. Ben. His patients. Ben.

"Hello." A young woman's voice told him that Dr. Chez was in. Would he like to leave a message?

No, he wouldn't. If he didn't do this here and now...

"I know he's otherwise occupied, but could you tell him that Donovan Barrett is on the phone."

"I—I'm sorry," the woman said. "But—"

"I'm a colleague." A lie. He wasn't that anymore.

She went away. In a moment the phone clicked to life.

"Don?" Phil's voice was incredulous.

"Hello, Phil, how are you?" What inconsequential nonsense. He and Phil had gone to med school together. They had danced at each other's weddings. He had thrown Phil out of his house when his friend had tried to get him to come back to work. Donovan had sent him a curt and formal apology in writing and had received a written acceptance in return. They hadn't spoken since.

"I'm fine. Great, Don. And...you?"

Donovan felt a lump form in his throat. "I'm fine, Phil," he said, trying to inject enthusiasm into his voice. "Really. Thank you for asking."

He could almost hear Phil expelling a sigh of relief. "It's good to hear you."

"Same here, buddy. But hey, I know it's a workday for you. You've got patients, and I have questions."

"You're coming back to the hospital." The hope in Phil's voice hit Donovan. How many people had he harmed or disappointed these past few years? He didn't know. He knew he had raged. He remembered yelling, pounding things, throwing things, cursing fate. He remembered telling Phil to get the hell out of his business and out of his life.

"I—no, I'm afraid I can't come back," Donovan said suddenly.

A pause. "Is there a medical problem, Don? Do you need help?"

Donovan took a deep breath. "Not medical, no, but yes, I could use help. By that, I mean that I know someone, a friend, who is considering adoption. I want to make sure that things go smoothly, that the details are tended to. I need avenues, information, someone who's kept on top of the latest legislation and knows the ins and outs and can help me help her."

"Adoption, Don? You said this was for…"

"For a friend," Donovan clarified. For a minute he was sure that Phil thought he had lost it, that he was going to try and adopt a child to replace Ben who was…utterly irreplaceable.

"She's my housekeeper, Phil, and yes, she's a friend. I'm not interested in adopting any children. I can't, but maybe I need a cause, a chance to do something good."

"You spent years doing good, Don."

"Yes, I did. But I took it too far. It cost me too much. I can't go there again, Phil. Don't ask it. Just…can you help me with this? Open some doors, find out a few things. I guess what I'm asking is…would you? I don't deserve your help but I'm asking."

Phil laughed, a harsh, barking laugh. "Shut up, Don. You think because you threw me out when you were going through total hell that I would hold that against you? I've missed you. I've worried about you, and I've only stayed away because I thought that was what you wanted."

It *was* what he'd wanted. Going back in any way was a danger to his sanity. He'd only called today because of Anna, but…

"I've missed you, too," Donovan said, and he realized he meant it. Looks like he owed Anna more than she knew.

"As for the info, I'll see what I can come up with. I haven't had much experience with adoptions over the years."

"Me either, but I thought you might know someone who had."

"I'll see what I can do. I'll give you a call if you tell me how to reach you and give me some information on the prospective adoptive parent."

"Thanks," Donovan said as he rattled off his number and address and gave Anna a glowing recommendation. "I owe you, Phil."

"You don't. We're friends, Don. Right? Still?"

"Still," Donovan agreed as he said his goodbyes.

He hung up the phone and looked out the window once again at those piers connecting water and land. A bridge, just like Anna. If she hadn't come into his life he would never have called Phil.

Of course, given the fact that he had no intention of going back to his old life, he wasn't sure if this process of reconnecting was a good thing or a bad thing.

But maybe the way she got him to do things even

when she wasn't trying to was just an Anna thing, something unique like her sunny ways, her concern for others or her lips that made him crave another taste.

Donovan slammed his palm down on the desk. He regretted that last thought. One slip regarding Anna's lips had him recalling how it had felt to touch her and to have her mouth opening beneath his.

"Damn!" Donovan stood up, pushing away from his desk and, hopefully, away from the direction his thoughts had been roaming. He was getting far too interested in his housekeeper. If he continued in this manner, he was bound to set off another disaster.

His relationship with Anna had to be a professional one. There were lines he couldn't cross.

"Set up some barriers and create some distance," he ordered himself. That task would at least keep him occupied with thoughts of something other than Anna's pretty lips. He hoped.

Her life here with Donovan was turning into a tango, Anna thought a few days later. When he entered a room she all but waltzed backward from it. When they ended up in the same space, they circled each other warily. The sheer physical energy of the two of them in the same place practically made the walls vibrate.

"I saw Donovan in town the other day," Bridget had told her just that morning. "Somehow I kept myself from salivating, but, Anna, he's even hotter than I thought. How can you be in the same room with him without bursting into flames?"

"It's not like that with us," Anna had said. "Donovan and I have a professional relationship."

But just this minute she had walked in on him reading the newspaper in the library and she knew that her words were a total lie.

Halting just inside the room, her duster in hand, Anna started to excuse herself and leave. The newspaper rattled and she noticed the way his fingers splayed over the pages. He had such wonderful hands.

Heat rose within her even though the day wasn't all that warm. "Excuse me," she said. "I'll come back later."

"No."

She stopped and stared at him.

He raised a brow, a hint of a smile playing over his lips.

"No?" she asked.

Shrugging, he stepped closer. "Forgive me. Make that no, please. I didn't mean to be so direct."

And she hadn't meant to stare at him as if she wanted to do more than dust the room. Anna stared at the feather duster. "This can definitely wait," she said as much to herself as to him.

"I need to talk to you. Why don't you have a seat?"

Uh-oh. She swallowed nervously.

"Don't look like that."

"Like what?"

"As if you think I'm going to devour you or fire you."

Anna sat. She waited, wishing she could figure out something productive to do with her hands. She hated being this way. Nervous. Indecisive. She raised her chin.

"Maybe you'd better just tell me what you want. I like men who are direct."

He looked slightly taken aback, but then a slow smile came to his face. "Okay, let's be direct. I've been making the rounds of everyone else's parties. It's time I reciprocated. I'd like to invite a small group of people over this weekend. Can we handle it?"

No, she wanted to say. Being a housekeeper was one thing. Organizing an event designed to impress people who belonged in a world where she would always be a servant was something a million times different. But she had practically begged Donovan to give her this job. She couldn't quit now.

"How many?" she asked.

"A dozen?"

"No problem." Those were her words, but her thoughts were something more akin to *oh, no!* "I'll just need to get some information from you. Linette and Clyde and John and I will take care of everything. Have you already issued invitations?"

Those slashing brows nearly joined when he frowned. "You think I'd ask people without first making sure you were prepared to do this?"

She couldn't keep from smiling then. "Donovan, you're the employer. I'm here to do your bidding. I'm sure that a man who has grown up with servants knows that."

"It's not the same."

Now she was the one frowning. "Because I'm inexperienced."

"Yes."

Anna got up and began to pace. "Do you have any complaints about my job performance?"

He stepped up beside her, matching his gait to hers. "Absolutely none."

She executed a quick turn. He stayed right with her. "Do you anticipate that I might not be up to seeing to the needs of a dozen people, even if they're rich and used to the best?"

"No, I don't. I known damn well that if I asked you to fly you would somehow manage to do it."

She started to turn again.

Donovan placed his arm around her waist and spun her around so that she was facing him. Because she had been moving when he caught her, her momentum sent her tumbling against his chest. She gazed up into his eyes, feeling his heart beating against her skin.

"I wasn't insulting you, Anna," he said, his voice low. "I would never do that. But the truth is that you and I have never sat down and ironed out your job description. I've been thinking about that. I know how much you need the work and why. And I don't want to inadvertently take advantage of you by asking you to do too much, because I'm pretty sure that whatever I ask you'll do your best to comply. That's a bit too one-sided. You need to be protected."

"From you?"

He loosened his hold and she took a visible breath. "I didn't mean in that way," she said. "I wasn't implying that you were taking advantage of me."

"And yet I have." His eyes darkened.

She shook her head. "No. Are you afraid you've asked too much of me as an employee, because if that's the case, you'd be wrong. You haven't asked. I've taken the initiative."

"I know that, but I haven't stopped you."

She had to smile at that. "Do you really think that you could?"

Donovan crossed his arms. He studied Anna for such a long time that she felt dizzy. "I think I could," he finally said.

He was right. She'd known all along that he was the one with the power. "But you haven't," she said slowly, "because you know how much I need this job."

"That wouldn't excuse me for letting you do too much. How about if we agree to this? I'll promise that your job is secure. You agree that if you're ever feeling overwhelmed, you'll let me know."

"And what will you do then?"

"I'll hire someone to help you."

"I couldn't let you do that."

Donovan stepped closer. He placed one finger beneath her chin, tilting her face up so that she was staring into his eyes. "You wouldn't have a choice, Anna. I'm the one in charge here."

His gaze was almost overwhelming. She wanted to lean closer. But then the meaning of his words shot through her.

Donovan was her boss. He *was* in charge. She was only his employee, and he had just made that abundantly clear.

"Do you understand, Anna? I won't let you sacrifice yourself." He let her go then, and took two steps backward, but he continued to study her. "Anna?"

She raised her chin. "I understand. You're the employer. I will, of course, let you know if I require help in order to do my job correctly."

"Good." His voice was harsh. He turned on one heel and left the room.

Anna let out a breath. She somehow found the wall and leaned against it. Her body sagged as reality hit, and she realized that ever since Donovan had come here, no matter what she'd told herself, she had not truly allowed herself to accept the chasm that stood between them.

He *was* her employer. He lived in a different world than she did. She was his to direct, and even if there was a physical attraction between them, there would always be a gaping cultural divide as well. A career divide. A life divide.

Donovan had made that clear.

Shame rushed through Anna. Somewhere inside, like it or not, she had harbored fantasies about him. She had dreamed about him. Even though she had known that there could never be anything between them, she had given in to those fantasies, however reluctantly. Now, even that had to stop. Allowing those dreams to continue could only hurt her and harm the future of her child. Her only goal right now had to be fulfilling her duties. She had a party to organize. It was imperative that she keep her mind off the man who was giving the party.

"It's for the best," she whispered to herself. Someday,

once some time had passed, Donovan might end up married to one of the guests at this party. She needed to start acting accordingly. From now on her attitude toward him would have to change. In every way.

With great effort, she tried not to think about who might be on Donovan's guest list. Instead she simply waited.

CHAPTER NINE

IF HE hadn't already felt like a jerk, his latest behavior with Anna would have cemented the title, Donovan thought. He had wanted to set up some barriers so he wouldn't be tempted to give in to the desire he felt for her, so he'd come up with the idea for this damned party. He'd thought it might create distance. Then, to keep her from running herself ragged planning the event, he'd pulled rank on her.

That had been totally unfair and arrogant. Because even if she was his employee, he had never really thought of her in those terms. He had plenty of employees, but Anna was different. From the minute he'd met her he'd known she was different. That had always been the problem.

"So, you acted like a pompous idiot and now she's playing by the rules you've set."

Ever since their conversation several days ago, Anna had been unfailingly professional. She had smiled politely; she had cleaned; she had organized and had treated him just the way any housekeeper would treat her employer. With distance and deference and respect and not an ounce of nosiness or stubbornness or spontaneous sunshine.

There had been no more humming or singing, no cute T-shirts, no acts of random impulsiveness like the time she had washed his car last week and had ended up totally and adorably soaked but triumphant. She had eliminated all the little things that had inadvertently, but constantly, brought her to his attention.

A frown drew Donovan's brows together. He supposed he should be ecstatic. In other circumstances, he would be, but he knew that Anna's natural tendency was to hum and sing and enjoy her work. He had silenced her, and she'd voiced not a word of complaint. She still seemed to like her job. So why was he feeling so ill-tempered?

He probably didn't really want to know the answer to that question. It might be incriminating. It would probably lead him to thoughts of Anna's lips. Still, he hated the fact that he'd somehow squelched her brightness.

"So go apologize—tell her you were wrong," he ordered himself.

But then…

Donovan blew out a breath.

"Every time you do something personal like that, you end up touching her." And if he gave in and touched her again, he might take things too far. Right now she was silencing her songs because she felt it was what the job required, but if he lost his self-control with her when he had nothing to offer, he'd end up hurting her for real. He might silence her songs for good.

There wasn't a way out of this that wouldn't be bad for Anna. Tonight was the party. After that...

Maybe he should start thinking of moving elsewhere, for Anna's sake, giving her permanent work here and a set of rooms so she could have space for her child. The place would need a caretaker if he wasn't here.

If he left, her life could get back to normal.

And he...

Could live anywhere. It didn't matter.

He only hoped that was true. He already had his memories of Ben haunting him. He couldn't have Anna haunting him, too.

Donovan was still reminding himself of that hours later when he descended to the first floor to greet his guests.

The uniform made her nervous, Anna conceded, as she and John circled the room handing out drinks and hors d'oeuvres. She couldn't remember ever having worn a uniform in her life other than for gym class, but it had just seemed like the right thing to do. She didn't want any of Donovan's friends noticing her or questioning him for being too soft on his employees.

The man had dared look askance when she had come up to him wearing the black skirt, white blouse and apron.

For the first time in the past few days she had frowned at him. "It's important to set the right tone," she reminded him. "You're trying to impress your guests."

For the first time in the past few days a hint of a devilish smile had played about his lips. "I am?"

She tried to frown harder. "Yes," she said firmly,

refusing to say more. If she took this further, he might end up not only smiling but laughing as well, and both his smile and his laugh did awful, wonderful things to her insides.

Anna refused to think about Donovan's smile. She went to the kitchen, gave Linette and John last minute instructions and tried to keep busy herself so that she wouldn't hyperventilate. If she hadn't done this right, if things didn't go well...

The correct next thought was *I might be fired,* but she wasn't really worried about that. For all that Donovan had been forced to remind her of their positions, she knew he wasn't a vindictive man. No, it was him she was worried about. He was starting a new life here. If she goofed things up for him, he would be hurt.

"Let's do this right," she said out loud.

"I promise not to drop anything or spill anything."

She blinked and turned around. John was standing there. She couldn't help smiling. "Believe me, John, I'm much more worried about doing something wrong myself. You're the experienced one. You have to lead the way and I'll follow."

A look of gratitude brightened his face. "You and Mr. Barrett are the best. He already found me today and told me not to worry." He laughed.

"He did?"

John nodded. "He also told me that if I had to spill something, I might consider aiming for Ms. Williams."

Anna widened her eyes.

Immediately John blushed. "Not that I would, Anna.

I wouldn't do a thing to embarrass him, not after he took such a risk hiring me."

Anna patted his sleeve. "I'm sure he didn't feel that he was taking a risk, John."

"I know. He said so, but still...I'll do my best by him."

And so will I, Anna promised herself after John had gone.

She put her best, maid-of-the-moment face on, picked up a tray and followed John out into the high-ceilinged room where Donovan was entertaining his guests.

Anna had decorated the gold room with white candles and yellow roses. The candlelight flickered off the walls, playing against the brass and crystal chandelier and highlighting the carved molding of the beautiful, spacious room.

The room, lovely though it was, was nothing compared to the guests. The men all wore crisp black and white and the women were mostly in black or white as well. Like beautiful marble chess pieces, Anna couldn't help thinking and then instantly felt awful. These people lived in a world different from her own, but that didn't mean they didn't have feelings and dreams and desires.

She held out her tray to an elderly man.

"Thank you very much," he said, taking a glass.

Anna mumbled a "you're welcome" and moved on, serving guests and being thanked at times. It seemed as if things would go all right, after all. Everyone seemed to like Donovan and he was being the perfect host.

She noticed his glass was empty. John had gone back

to the kitchen to refill his tray. Realizing that she would have to do the honors, Anna's breath caught in her throat. She had served Donovan many times in the past few weeks but somehow sidling up to him in this company seemed different. It made her feel exposed, as if anyone might look into her face and see that she was attracted to her employer.

Ridiculous. She was no longer attracted to Donovan. At least she didn't intend to allow herself to be. And she had a job to do.

She walked up to him and held out her tray.

"Thank you, Anna," he said, taking the glass and looking directly at her.

Oh, wasn't it just like him to do that? He wouldn't want her to feel like a piece of furniture and so he would call her by name and look at her. Didn't he know that wasn't the way it was done? At least she didn't think it was. He probably knew much more about the process than she did.

"You're welcome, Mr. Barrett," she said, starting to move away, but she was still distracted by her thoughts and Donovan's nearness. For a second, her foot caught on the shoe of the person standing behind her. For what seemed like forever, Anna teetered.

Donovan's arm shot out. He steadied the tray, and with his other arm he steadied Anna, his hand at her waist.

She sucked in a breath. To her own ears it sounded loud, like a gasp. She knew her eyes widened.

"Are you all right?" Donovan murmured.

Quickly she righted herself. "Yes, I'm fine, thank you,"

she murmured and somehow gave away the rest of the glasses of wine and found her way back to the kitchen.

She had lied. She wasn't fine. The instant Donovan's hand had rested on her waist, she had felt positively dizzy in a way she hadn't when she was merely trying to get her balance.

"That must have been some grip you had on her, Donovan," she heard a woman's voice murmur. "She looked as if you had just invited her into your bed. What's that about?"

"Oh, shut up, Kendra," another woman said. Anna recognized the voice as that belonging to Susannah McGraff, a gorgeous and intelligent woman whose family had made a fortune in department stores. "Anna was clearly just embarrassed because she knew everyone had seen her stumble. You would have felt the same. Any of us would have."

"Absolutely," another voice said. Anna recognized it as the elderly man's. "Thank you, John," he continued, and Anna was glad that John, at least, was surviving the evening.

But she couldn't hide in the kitchen forever. Linette was putting food on the trays and John had just told Donovan it was time to go into the dining room.

Anna waited to give everyone time to get seated. Then she and John picked up their trays and prepared to serve. With a little luck the evening and her ordeal would be over soon.

CHAPTER TEN

DONOVAN'S heart flipped when he looked up and saw Anna standing in the doorway carrying a tray that looked as if it weighed almost as much as she did. He'd been aware all night that she was nervous, and he was pretty sure she was afraid she'd somehow spoil his party.

Damn him for not making it clear that this party didn't matter. The only point of this affair had been to stop spending so much time thinking about Anna.

He'd wanted to remind himself that he and Anna couldn't be together. This party had merely been a diversion. But, somehow, he'd messed up the message, and here she was struggling to create the appearance that she'd been hauling heavy trays around all her life.

She took a step into the room.

He should stay seated. She wouldn't thank him for calling attention to her.

She took another step, her head high. He knew she was strong, but the tray was completely laden. Her body wasn't meant to take this kind of punishment.

Muttering beneath his breath, Donovan stood. He rose to meet her.

Her eyes widened. He saw her mouth the word *no*.

He frowned and leaned close enough to take the tray. "You promised you'd get help if you needed it," he said, his voice pitched low and meant for her ears only.

"I'm fine," she said.

"You're trembling."

"This doesn't look good for either of us."

"Too bad. I'll fix it. You just smile," he commanded, taking the tray and carrying it the last few feet to the table.

"Can't lose the woman who keeps this house running, can I?" he asked his guests. "The gears would stop turning without Anna. My gardener says the flowers bloom just for her."

Her eyes widened. She gave him a shocked and flustered look. When she leaned in to take the first dish, he could almost swear that the word "liar" came to him on a breath of air, but that might have been his imagination.

Or maybe his conscience. Clyde did think Anna made the sun rise and set, but that last had been a bit of obvious exaggeration designed to make his actions seem understandable.

Not that it had worked. Kendra Williams was smiling knowingly and it was obvious that she would be spreading petty gossip tomorrow. He probably shouldn't have invited her. He might have done it just so John could gloat a bit. Even Susannah was looking at him with a question in her eyes. As well as a hint of admiration.

She *was* an attractive and intelligent and good-hearted woman. A man would be a fool not to try to win at least her lust. But he looked at her and saw only a friend. His heart didn't flip.

Still, he made an effort to smile at her and to engage the rest of his guests. For Anna's sake he didn't call attention to her again that evening. She stayed away, and they didn't speak to each other except in the most necessary of instances.

The minute the door closed behind his last guest, however, and John and Linette had gone home, he headed for the kitchen. Anna was there putting things away, bent over a cabinet, her beautifully rounded bottom in the air.

Donovan groaned.

Anna whirled. "I didn't know you were there."

"I'm here," he said simply. He didn't try for more, because what he was thinking was that he was glad the guests were gone and he was alone with her. She wouldn't want to know that any more than he did.

She fiddled with the handle of a cabinet. "I think it went well tonight. Your guests seemed entranced by you."

"It went well," he agreed. "Thanks to you."

"You don't have to say that."

"It's true. You organized the whole thing. All I did was talk."

"And be yourself. People like you. That's important."

Probably it was to most people, but to him it wasn't anymore. He hadn't cared one bit what anyone in the room thought of him. All his thoughts had been focused on this lady.

"Thank you," he said.

She turned aside slightly, her hair brushing the curve of her jaw. "You shouldn't have helped me with the tray."

"It was heavy."

"You're not supposed to do those things. I am. You know that." She looked at him, taking a step forward. Her eyes flashed. He loved that.

"Are you lecturing me?"

Anna froze. He knew what she was going to say.

"I'm teasing, Anna."

"Maybe, but I *was* lecturing you. That can't be right."

He laughed. "It feels right."

She raised her chin. "You told me that you were the boss, that you were in charge, and you were right."

"I was a pompous jerk."

"Then go on being a jerk."

He shook his head. "You don't sing anymore."

"It seemed unprofessional."

"Then be unprofessional. I don't want you to change to fit some mold you think you should fit just because I tried to bully you."

She laughed at that, then. "Are you sure you were really a doctor?"

Her words stopped him cold. "Why?"

"Don't doctors have to give a lot of orders? To their receptionists and their nurses and their patients?" Her voice was soft. She gazed at him. "Don't answer that."

"Why?"

"Because you never talk about your past. It must hurt."

"It does and yet…yes, I gave orders, but only when

they were necessary. It doesn't seem to be necessary for you, Anna."

"Why not?"

He smiled sadly. "Because you have a tendency to do more than I would ask."

"Do you miss it? Being a doctor?"

Donovan thought about that. "I miss it, but I can't do it anymore. I don't want to. I gave everything to medicine and not enough to Ben. When he needed me most I wasn't there for him as a doctor or as a dad. I wasn't even with him the day that car came out of nowhere and took his life. I was working. He'd been visiting me but I sent him home with a friend instead of taking him myself. So, medicine is over for me. In a way, it robbed me of Ben. I can't help wondering what would have happened—or not happened—if I'd taken him home myself. Does that make sense?"

She nodded. "Yes. I suppose I can see why you would feel that way, anyway. I'm sorry about your son. Terribly sorry."

He took her hands. "Thank you. Me, too."

Anna looked down at her palms resting in his. For a minute she seemed to lean closer to him. Then she quickly pulled away.

"I'm sorry," she repeated, and he was pretty sure that she was apologizing for something else. Maybe even for wanting a child when he had lost his.

"It's okay," he said as she excused herself and left the room.

But it wasn't. It wasn't okay that he had lost Ben and

it wasn't okay that he was starting to ache for a woman who needed a child.

And he did ache. All night long he thought of her.

He wished he had done more than hold her hands. Yet he was grateful that she'd had the sense to pull away.

Next time…

"Don't let there be a next time," he warned himself. He hoped he would heed his own good advice.

The last thing Anna thought of when she went to bed that night was Donovan. The first thing she thought of when she woke up was Donovan, and she thought of him all day.

"Stop it!" she ordered herself, as if that was really going to help. The man had been in her thoughts since the moment she'd met him.

And last night…he'd looked like a dream. She'd wanted to warn the other women in the room away.

Ridiculous thought. Clearly he belonged to those women. He was one of them.

But when he'd taken the tray from her, his hands had touched hers for the briefest of seconds, and she'd thought the trembling in her knees would send her tumbling. How silly. Despite the fires that sprang to life when they got together, he had just been trying to help her.

She'd watched him last night. It was as if he had been untouched by what was going on around him. He had laughed and talked and charmed everyone. Yet he'd left his guests to help his housekeeper carry in a heavy tray. He wasn't as invested in the party as he should have been. She hadn't fully understood until they'd had that talk later. Then she realized what the problem was. There was nothing real in his life anymore. He'd left it all behind.

"There's no fixing that," she reminded herself. "It's his choice."

But she burned to do something to help him, to bring a little life and happiness back to him. Just for a short time.

"And you know what that means?" she grumbled to herself. "It means you're in too deep. You need to back away, to keep your distance from him."

Yes, and that was just what she intended to do. Keep her distance.

Three days later, Anna was starting to feel as if her nerves were completely shot. Because she didn't want Donovan to feel bad she had gone back to her usual methods of keeping the house under control. She'd resumed her humming and singing, but in truth, it was hard. If she sang too loudly, the man might slip into the room and if he did that, she wasn't completely sure she could trust herself to behave normally and not reveal the fact that she wanted to beg him to kiss her again.

The final straw came when she was scrubbing the tiled floor of the hallway. She worked her way down the hall until she found herself in the doorway of the sunroom.

A sound caught her attention. She looked up to find herself staring straight into Donovan's eyes.

"I thought you were in the library."

"I was." But obviously he wasn't anymore.

Anna tried not to think about the fact that she was on her hands and knees, that her clothes were damp and clingy or that she was staring up into Donovan's eyes.

He frowned. "I don't think I pay you nearly enough to do that."

She gave him "the look," the one that brooked no argument. "You pay me plenty."

"You never said you were going to turn yourself into a scrubwoman. There's got to be a better way."

"There are numerous ways. This one works best. The grout needs cleaning."

"Then we'll get rid of the grout." ·

She sat back in a kneeling position, her hands on her hips. "That would be a waste of money and this beautiful tile."

"The tile is immaterial. Get up off your knees, Anna." His eyes were dark.

Her heart skipped a beat. Oh, who was she kidding? Her heart skipped so many beats that had she been in a doctor's office, he would have called for an EKG.

Anna's first instinct was to argue. She knew what cleaning a house entailed, and it was her job. "Donovan, I—"

She had barely opened her mouth when he was across the room, reaching for her. His big hands found her waist and he easily tugged her to her feet. Dropping the cloth she was holding, Anna stumbled, falling farther into Donovan's grasp.

"You're very bossy," she whispered weakly, embarrassed by her awkwardness and by her reaction to him.

"I know," he said, slipping one hand beneath her hair and cupping her head. He gazed down at her, studying her as if he'd never seen someone like her before. "It's my job."

Then he lowered his head and covered her lips with his own.

Anna's reaction was immediate and involuntary. She pushed her hands up his back and rose on her toes. Straining against him, she tilted her head to give him better access to her mouth. As if he needed help. Donovan was kissing her over and over. Nibbling, biting, licking.

"You make me crazy," he said, his voice harsh. "I think about you too much, all the time. I imagine other men touching you because I know I shouldn't be touching you at all."

He kissed her again.

"Yes," she said on a breath. She returned his kiss. "No. I mean no. I shouldn't be kissing you like this. We don't belong. We don't fit."

She pressed her palms against his chest to push away but ended up leaving them there, breathing in his scent, turning her head to feel more of him as he nibbled his way from her lips to her jaw, down her neck.

Anna shivered in his arms. "I'm not like this," she said, whether to Donovan or herself, she didn't know. And yet she *was* like this. With him.

"I know. I know. Do you think I don't know that?" His lips scorched the side of her neck, made her ache. She twisted, trying to get closer to him. "I know darn well I should stay away from you, for your sake. I don't want to hurt you. I really don't want to hurt you, Anna."

And, as if the truth of his words finally struck home, Donovan took a long, shuddering breath and set her away from him.

He studied her with dark, tortured eyes. He had done things and failed to do things in his life that filled him with regret. Anna knew that. Now she was one of those things, and she hated that, even though he was right about the fact that he could hurt her.

"It's okay," she finally managed to say, struggling to raise her voice from a weak whisper to a firm and affirmative and somewhat normal sound. She failed. "I'm all right," she reiterated, succeeding a bit better this time.

"How can you be all right?" he asked angrily. "This isn't the first time we've done this. It's not what any woman should have to accept from her employer."

Anna blinked, her eyes opening wide. "You think that was what I was doing? Accepting and fostering the advances of my employer because I need work?"

He made a slashing movement with his hand, cutting her off. "Of course not. I think I know you better than that. What I meant was—"

Now she was the one stopping his speech by holding up her hand. "I know what you meant. You meant that you hold all the cards, the power, the money and I'm at your mercy. You're suggesting that I might be unwilling."

His brows drew together and he didn't respond.

Anna sighed. "You're not saying anything because

you know that I wasn't at all unwilling. I've told you that I'm attracted to you."

"Yes, and knowing that, I should never have taken advantage. A good employer doesn't do that."

"You don't get to define being a good employer. I'm the employee. I get to decide."

He let out a groan. "I hardly think that you were looking for a boss who would back you up against a wall and put his hands and lips on you."

As worried and chagrined and afraid of her own emotions as she was, Anna couldn't keep from smiling just a little. "No, I don't think that would have been on my list of desirable attributes, but…it happened."

"Because I stepped over the line."

"And because I followed you eagerly."

Donovan stared directly into her eyes. "It would be best if you refrained from revealing such things to me right now. I don't trust myself."

"But I do," she said softly. "At a time when you wanted to move ahead to the next step, you stopped, and if I'm not mistaken it was for my sake more than for yours. Thank you."

Donovan leaned back against the wall. "Don't thank me. It's all I can do to keep my hands to myself right now. It's very important that I do that, too. I can't hurt you, Anna. I can't."

"I know that," she admitted, softly. "And you're right. It's wrong for us to touch. I trust you, and I haven't trusted a man in a long time."

His eyes came open. "Why?" He looked suddenly

alert in a way he hadn't been before. The agony was gone from his eyes. This was the man who cared about people so much that he forgot his own needs and hurts.

Because he was that kind of man, Anna opted to tell him some things she had told very few people in her life. "I may have mentioned that my father deserted my mother and me when I was little. There's nothing all that unusual in that. It happens all the time, but it did affect the way I thought of men. I think I was a bit too eager to be liked, perhaps less discerning than I should have been. Several times I got involved with boys or men who turned out to be less interested in me than they had pretended to be. They wanted more from me than I was willing to give and they lied to obtain my compliance."

Donovan swore.

Anna shook her head. "I was naive, but not that naive. When it became obvious that I was being used, I walked away. Less trusting and less rosy-eyed but unscathed physically. At least until I met Brent. He was intelligent and funny, and he didn't rush me. I fell like a rock. I loved him. We were supposed to be married. I was honest with him about the fact that I couldn't have children. I moved to Chicago to be with him. At first, he seemed happy, but as the wedding grew closer, he began to withdraw. He started to say cruel things to me. Eventually he threw my childlessness in my face. It seems that while I was planning my move to Chicago he was busy meeting someone else, someone who could give him the children he had suddenly decided he had to have. At least that was what he said. I'm not sure the truth had anything to do with my childbearing abilities. I think…I think he just used that as an excuse and I think he knew he wanted out before I ever made the move. His lies and defection…I guess it was the last straw."

Total silence greeted her words. A clock ticked loudly in the next room.

"So you came home."

She looked away, unable to continue to meet his gaze. The truth made her sound so pathetic.

"Yes. Where else would I go?" There had been nowhere. No one, but she couldn't say that.

"Anna," Donovan groaned. "Come here."

No, she was too vulnerable right now. She should never have told. He was probably pitying her. She shook her head.

"Anna. Please. I won't touch you if you don't want me to."

But, of course she did want him to touch her. Still. Even after remembering how foolish she had been in the past. That was the awful thing.

She sighed and moved closer. He kept his hands at his side. "I wish I had known you then," he said.

Anna raised her chin. "Why?"

"So I could beat up that scumbag for you. You should have had a champion."

"I did. I had myself."

Donovan smiled then. "So you did."

"I didn't tell you this so you would feel sorry for me."

"I don't feel sorry for you. I admire you. You got kicked in the heart but you came away from it and made something of yourself. You turned things around. I've always admired you and now I have one more good reason."

She smiled and shook your head. "I told you," she said, as if he hadn't spoken, "so that you would know that you can't hurt me that way. I've been hurt by unfeeling men. That's not you."

He opened his mouth.

She pressed her fingers against it, struggling to ignore his warm breath on her fingertips. "You've touched me," she said, "but you've always been truthful with me. You never led me to believe there could or would be anything more than desire. I appreciate that, because you and I both know we could never have a future. If you'd promised me rainbows or happily ever afters I would respect you so much less."

He raised one dark brow. "You wouldn't believe me, then?"

Her heart sighed but she smiled. "No, I wouldn't. I've learned a lot since the days of Brent. Actually I suppose I owe him a debt of gratitude, since he greatly simplified my life."

Donovan scowled. "He turned you off of men."

Anna removed her fingertips from Donovan's lips and gave him a quick kiss that sent sizzles straight down to her toes. "No, he turned me off of wanting to get seriously involved with men. I still like to kiss them now and then."

She started to spin away. Donovan caught her wrist and pulled her to him. "Do you kiss a lot of men?"

Just you, she wanted to say. *You're the only one I want to kiss.*

But almost immediately Donovan let her go. "Forget I asked that," he said. "It's none of my business."

His eyes still smoldered, and Anna realized her mistake. She hadn't wanted to hurt him, but her flippant comment had done so. Because he was trying to do the right thing, and she was only making it more difficult. For both of them.

"Forget I said that," she said. "It wasn't appropriate, and it wasn't really true. I should get back to business."

Donovan gave a quick nod and let her go. Anna had the terrible feeling that she would never feel the touch of his lips again. She should be happy about that.

But instead she knew that she would dream about his kisses for a great many years to come. Starting tonight.

CHAPTER ELEVEN

WHEN Donovan emerged from his bedroom the next morning, he heard a voice at the front door. Whispering. Or what might pass as whispering to a boy, he supposed. He recognized the voice immediately. Frank. And since the voice was followed by what sounded like silence he assumed that Anna was there, too, talking too quietly to hear.

The fact that she was talking that quietly concerned Donovan. Anna wasn't a whisperer. If she had lowered her voice, then something was worrying her.

Immediately Donovan turned toward the front of the house. His first instinct might be to shy away from contact with children, but if something was worrying Anna, then he was going to see if he could help.

He quickly made his way to the top of the stairs, his feet silent on the thick carpeting. But there he stopped. Downstairs Anna and Frank were seated cross-legged in the front hallway staring at something Frank held in his hands.

"See, I just ride the thing. I don't know how to fix it," Frank was saying, the frustration apparent in his voice.

"Shh, you'll wake Donovan," Anna said, and Frank immediately blushed.

"Sorry, I forgot."

She stopped looking at what she was holding and turned to Frank. "It's okay. I didn't mean to embarrass you. I just…it's just…"

"I know. Everybody knows about Mr. Barrett's kid. My mom says I have to learn to be more sensitive, but I don't know. If I had a kid and he died, I wouldn't want everyone to act like he had never even been born."

Donovan's heart clenched. He had to concentrate on making sure he didn't gasp or worse. Frank's words, low as they had been, echoed in his ears.

"I know, sweetie," Anna was saying softly. "It's hard to understand, but that's the way adults are at times. The pain of losing a child is so great that it's almost unbearable. Not thinking about it is the only way of coping."

Forcing himself to keep breathing as normally as possible, Donovan thought about what he'd heard. That this child and this woman should be trying so hard to protect him…that they were so concerned they tiptoed around him…

Donovan closed his eyes and took a deep breath. He was half-tempted to slip backward into his room. That would be the sensitive thing to do. It would save Frank and Anna embarrassment and distress. But it would also allow their attempt to wrap him in protective cotton to continue. That wasn't fair to either Anna or Frank. They shouldn't have to be nervous about saying the wrong thing in front of him for fear it would bring up bad memories about Ben.

As if the very thought had been too much, Donovan's next breath conjured up a memory of Ben's ready smile. He could almost feel his little boy's fingers enclosed in his hand as they walked down the street together. Ben's birthday was coming up soon. His child had loved birthdays.

Intense pain swirled with a warm and sweet sadness.

"If you had a kid, what would you do if it died?" Frank was asking.

"I don't know," Anna said sadly. "I guess, like Donovan, I have some things I almost can't bear to think about."

"My mom says that even if I'm a lot of trouble, she couldn't get along without me," Frank said. "And that's why I need to be sensitive with Mr. Barrett."

This was the wrong time to step in, Donovan knew. The boy was going to be horrified, but if he didn't…

Donovan descended the stairs, making as much noise as possible.

Frank looked up, his big eyes round, his mouth a hollow O that emitted no sound. Red crept up beneath his T-shirt, coloring his neck and his face and especially the tips of his ears. Immediately the boy looked down.

Donovan almost reached out a hand to console him even though he wasn't anywhere near Frank yet. He clattered down the last of the stairs, turning his attention to Anna.

Immediately she rose to her feet, her mouth open, although she didn't speak. No doubt she was trying to come up with something soothing to say. More likely she was going to say she was sorry.

Something hot and dark and red and very much like anger slithered through Donovan. He didn't want her to speak, not if she was going to apologize. He suddenly hated all the things that stood between them, most especially her position as his underling that seemed to demand she be submissive and careful and distant.

"It's fine," he said quietly. "It's all right."

"I'm sorry," she said. There, she'd done it. He wanted to rant, to rave, to kiss the "I'm sorry" right out of her.

Donovan sighed. Telling her he was fine obviously wasn't going to do the trick and make her feel less terrible. And it wasn't going to make Frank feel any better, either.

"Look," he said. "It's beyond tough losing a child, but friends shouldn't have to pretend Ben's death didn't happen. It did, and nothing will bring him back. And Frank is right. Despite the fact that it hurts like hell to think of Ben, pretending he never existed is worse. It's only natural for you to talk about what happened."

Donovan didn't know if what he was saying made sense or even if it was true. All he knew at the moment was one thing. "I don't want either of you to feel bad for talking about the fact that I once had a son and I don't anymore."

Frank raised his head slightly, but he still looked horribly uncomfortable. Of course, there was no reason for him to feel comfortable. Donovan was a total stranger, and death was never a comfortable topic. A man couldn't expect a boy to break the ice, no matter the circumstances.

Donovan dropped to a squat. He held out his hand. "That looks like a bike chain. Mind if I have a look?"

"You know how to fix bikes?" Anna asked, a surprised look in her eyes.

A chuckle escaped Donovan, but before he could speak Frank let out a loud whoosh that lifted his bangs. "Anna, he fixes people. Probably bikes are easier."

"Sometimes they are," Donovan said, taking the greasy chain Frank held out to him. "Not always. I'm not an expert on bike repair, but this looks like something I can handle. One of the links needs to be bent and oiled. I doubt there's a chain tool here, but if I'm careful, a hammer, nail and a block of wood will do the trick and allow me to separate the chain so I can fix it. Come on. Let's go see what's in the garage."

"You're going to get all greasy," Anna admonished.

Donovan flashed her a grin and tweaked her nose with his thumb. "I know. Grease is part of the deal when you're taking a bike apart. If you don't get dirty, what fun is it? Right?"

He looked at Frank.

"Oh, yeah," Frank agreed. "It's a guy thing, Anna."

Anna squealed and looked as if she'd just swallowed the chain.

"Uh-oh," Donovan said. "That probably wasn't the best thing to say, Frank. Anyway, Anna's no slouch with tools herself, you know?"

"You mean like an honorary guy?"

Anna crossed her arms. "I am not an honorary guy, I'll have you know."

Frank was starting to get that flustered, red-faced look again. Donovan knew he had to take pity on him. By the look Anna flashed him, he was sure she felt the same.

"Let's just say that Anna's a woman who happens to be talented in many areas. Fixing bikes is not a guy or a woman thing," Donovan told Frank.

Frank gave Anna a sideways tentative glance.

"That was very tactful of you," Anna told Donovan. "A good thing to keep in mind when dealing with girls, Frank," she said. "We don't like to be put in boxes."

Frank looked disgusted. "I'm not ready to start *dealing* with girls, yet, Anna," he told her. "Especially not Mitzi Ronberg."

Anna stopped in her tracks. She gave Frank a speculative glance, like a mother who hadn't realized her baby was growing up. Donovan did his best not to laugh. He had no idea who Mitzi Ronberg was, but he was willing to bet the young lady in question had her heart set on Frank.

"Well, of course not," Anna said, as they resumed their walk and opened the door of the garage where tools and a workbench were kept. "I meant down the road. No rush at all, and anyway, thank you for even thinking that I could be an honorary man. It was very thoughtful of you."

Frank shrugged and smiled. "No problem. I'll remember about the 'no-boxes' thing, though. My mom would probably agree. Can you fix it?" he asked, turning to Donovan and making a swift change of subject.

How quickly young people moved on, Donovan thought. He envied Frank his ability to rebound as if nothing had happened. Despite the boy's obvious youth and that comment about Mitzi, he was, in some ways, wiser than many adults.

"We'll do all we can," Donovan promised.

Fortunately it didn't take long to fix the slightly damaged chain and get it back on the bike. Donovan wiped the grease off his hands and stood.

"I think it'll do," he said.

Frank tried it out, riding in a small circle. "Works great. You're the best, Mr. Barrett! Wait till I tell Mom that you were the one who fixed my bike. I think she has a crush on you. Of course, she says all the women do. I mean…you know what I mean."

"Even Anna?" Donovan couldn't resist.

Frank looked up. He stared at Anna as if such a thing could never have occurred to him. "Well, of course not. Anna works for you. You're her boss. She probably hates you sometimes. I hate my mom sometimes. I mean, not really, but still…I mean…"

"I know what you mean," Anna said, managing a smile. "And you're right. A woman can't have a crush on her boss. That would be a big mistake. How's the bike?"

"Perfect."

"So…don't you think you'd better deliver the rest of your papers before it gets late and your mother wonders where you are?"

"Guess so. Thanks, Mr. Barrett. See you, Anna."

Frank pedaled away.

"Thank you," Anna said softly.

Donovan turned and looked at her. "I didn't do much. It was a simple repair."

"You made him feel comfortable. And you didn't make fun of him, even after that comment about Mitzi."

"She have a thing for him?"

Anna shrugged. "She's a fashion doll wannabe. Nice, but pretty focused on boys right now. And Frank's a sweet kid."

"That's what girls want nowadays? Sweet kids?"

Laughing, Anna started to walk toward the house. "Okay, he's a bit of a bad boy. Gets in trouble at times, but he's not mean."

"Ah, bad boys. I see the world hasn't changed. Women are still chasing the ones who are all wrong for them."

The two of them stopped in their tracks. His comment had been flippant. He'd said it without even thinking, but it had been the wrong thing to say.

"Forget I said that," he said.

"Can't," she said. "Anyway, it was true. No need to be sorry." She continued moving toward the house.

"Going back to work?" he couldn't help asking.

She turned and walked backward, a big grin on her face. "I'm going to get your reward for being so nice to Frank and making his day."

"You're going to give me a reward?" he asked. Unbidden, a vision of Anna in his arms, in his bed, came to mind.

"Cake," she said with a look acknowledging the fact that she knew his thoughts had wandered into the forbidden. "You get chocolate cake. Linette makes the best."

Regret trickled through Donovan even though he knew she was right. Getting close was just prolonging the torture when they'd both agreed there wasn't any future for the two of them.

In fact, if he stayed in Lake Geneva, he might one day have to deal with a painful truth. Sooner or later some man might teach Anna that he could be trusted and that she could risk loving him.

There would be a man who could raise her child with her.

You'll have to see her with that man all the time, he told himself. Exchanging loving glances, maybe even touching. When that day comes, it's going to drive you out of your mind.

He took a deep breath. "I'm sure Linette makes great chocolate cake," he told Anna. "I'll be right in."

He would—somehow—manage to eat a slice of cake, smile and thank Anna and Linette. Then he was going out.

It was impossible to stay here today. He had to escape the confines of this house. Now that the raw truth was in the open, he needed some space, some time.

And in the long run?

Maybe Lake Geneva wasn't big enough for both Anna and himself. If one of them had to go, it would be him. This town was her world.

It was time to start thinking of what his next world would be.

CHAPTER TWELVE

Anna slid her little car into a coveted parking space near the edge of town and walked toward the shop where Bridget worked. She couldn't stay in the house anymore, not when every thought of Donovan was making her crazy and achy. Fortunately she had errands she could run in town, and Bridget and some friends had agreed to meet her for lunch.

Donovan had told her he was going to Williams Bay hours earlier, so maybe she could have a brief respite from pretending to be the perfect housekeeper when she was obviously so bad at it. Anna was pretty sure kissing one's employer or lusting after him was grounds for instant disqualification in the housekeeper hall of fame.

She really did not want to think about kissing or lusting now.

Breezing into the gift shop, Anna saw that Paula and Nan were already waiting. They greeted her with hugs.

It was a busy day at the shop, and all too soon Anna and her friends had eaten their lunch. Bridget would have to be getting back to work soon.

"You've been so quiet today," Nan told Anna. "You didn't even admonish me for any of my gibes about what you were doing with Donovan."

Anna managed a smile, but it wasn't a prizewinner. And obviously not very convincing, either.

"Oh," Paula said.

"What?" Anna couldn't control the quaver in her voice. Paula had a knack for seeing things a bit too clearly.

Her friend studied her carefully. "Nothing. We don't have much time left today. Let's walk. Have to burn the calories."

They started down the street and had gotten as far as the cruise line docks when Anna felt a twinge, a sense of heightened anticipation and awareness. She started to glance to the right…then quickly glanced away again. If she was right, and her friends saw what she thought she'd seen…

"Let's go this way," she said, attempting to turn in a different direction.

But her voice and actions had obviously given her away. Paula pivoted to the right. "Isn't that Donovan?"

"Probably not. He was going to Williams Bay," Anna said, but her mouth went dry as she looked up. Donovan was there, buying a ticket for one of the cruises.

"Looks like he's back from Williams Bay," Nan said. "Come on, let's go say hello."

"What? We can't do that," Anna said. "He's alone. By choice," she stressed. "Besides, Bridget has to get back to the shop. And you—"

"Have a few hours before work. Paula, too. Bridge?"

Bridget groaned. "I'd love to stay, but Anna's right. I'm gone. That doesn't mean I don't want a complete rundown of what happens here today. Anna, go on. Say hello. The man is a newcomer to our town and you're acting as if he's poison. That's just not right. Now, go over there and be pleasant."

"That's right, Anna. We should be extending our hospitality," Paula said. "Let's go. He looks lonely. Doesn't he, Nan?"

"It's a crime for a man like that to even walk down the street unaccompanied," Nan agreed.

Anna frowned. She looked from Bridget to Paula to Nan. "That's enough. Would all of you just stop? You're not fooling anyone. I see what you're trying to do, so let me tell you something. If Donovan wanted company, he would ask for it, and he'd have plenty of volunteers. You know that. Now I need to get back to work. I have duties."

"Yeah, well I think the house will manage to stay in one piece for a few hours even if you're not there to hold it together. Looks like Donovan is taking the full lake tour on the Walworth. He's alone. That can't be fun," Nan said, sweeping Anna along. "I'll bet he would like company."

Anna was pretty sure he wouldn't. He'd probably wonder why his housekeeper and her friends were crowding him when he was having some alone time.

"Absolutely not," she said, digging in her heels.

"Donovan," Paula called, waving her arm.

A groan escaped Anna's lips as Donovan turned around. For a second he frowned as if he couldn't understand what was happening. Then he started their way.

"You're going to pay," Anna muttered, quietly jabbing Paula in the back. "The man was alone because he wanted to be alone."

"But he's smiling." Nan said the words between her teeth.

"He smiles a lot. He has manners, unlike some people I know," Anna declared, stepping forward to meet Donovan.

"I'm sorry we disturbed you," she told him.

He shook his head. "You say that too much. Don't."

"Ooh, commanding. That's sooo sexy," Paula whispered.

Anna rammed her elbow backward slightly, surprising an oomph from her friend.

"I know, but you were just about to board. We shouldn't have interrupted you."

"You're not. I was just…looking for something to do, getting to know the area."

"A cruise is a great way to do that," Paula agreed. "Of course, so is a local."

Her friends were loyal and she loved them to death, but none of them was particularly subtle and it was obvious that they had gone beyond mere curiosity about Donovan to deciding that Anna needed to be matched up with him.

Somehow she managed to hang on to her teetering, pasted-on smile. "The tour is very thorough and a great way to see the community from a different perspective," she said. "I hope you enjoy it."

Donovan's eyes held a trace of amusement. "You

don't think I'm going to let this pass, do you? I have three locals here and you think I'm going to miss out on the opportunity to hear the secrets the other passengers don't get to hear?"

He tugged on her hand. She didn't budge. "Donovan, don't tell me you're not being pushed into this. Stop being so nice."

His grip tightened. "I'm not being nice. The truth is that after this morning, I did need some time alone. I went over to Williams Bay, had breakfast and spent some time at the water's edge watching the boats. It was only natural to segue from that into actually wanting to be out on the lake. I've heard it's calming."

It was, but Anna felt anything but calm right now.

"You don't have to do this, Donovan."

He gazed down at her and took her hands. "And you don't, either. This isn't a command or an order. It's not part of your job, but I'd like you to come along."

Anna studied his expression for several seconds. "Better decide soon," he urged. "The boat is leaving."

Reluctantly she agreed. She tried not to notice that Paula and Nan were all but high-fiving each other. Anna squirmed. She'd discuss this with her friends later. For now, she followed Donovan onto the boat.

"Inside or outside?" she asked, turning to him.

He held out his hand, motioning for her to lead the way. "After you. You're the expert."

"Upstairs, then. It's open air."

Together they moved up to the top level of the boat. "Anna," someone called out. She turned and saw

Thomas Liddell, a local real estate agent. He was with a young couple, probably showing them the sights, trying to close a deal.

"Hi, Tom," she said with a smile.

He nodded slightly to her right and she got the message. "Tom, this is Donovan Barrett, my boss. He owns Morning View Manor. You know where it is. Tom and I went to school together," she told Donovan.

"We worked at a local restaurant together, too," Tom reminded her. "For more than one summer."

For half a second, Donovan's hand tightened on her arm, but then he let her go.

"I understand you have a way with a bicycle chain," Tom said with a grin.

"You know Frank?" Donovan asked.

"Everyone knows Frank," Tom agreed. "He's got a big case of hero worship. I guess it's not every day that someone of your stature stoops to fixing a kid's bike."

Donovan held out his hands as if to ward off the praise. "No stature here. And the bike thing was mostly luck. I know one or two tricks."

"You bike?"

Anna felt rather than saw the way Donovan jerked slightly. "I used to. Now and then."

From his reaction, she wondered if he'd ridden with Ben in tow.

"Some great trails around here. I could use a companion. My wife doesn't like anything with less than four wheels," Tom said.

Anna turned to look up at Donovan and saw that his

expression had turned thoughtful, even surprised. "I might want to try that," he agreed.

Tom nodded. "Well, better get back to my clients. Nice meeting you, Donovan."

Tom moved away and Anna followed Donovan to a seat near the front of the boat.

"You're handy to have around," he said.

She blinked.

"I meet a lot of nice people when I'm with you," he said.

"Oh, that. Tom's just very friendly."

He hesitated for a second. "He wasn't one of the ones who hurt you, was he?"

"Tom? No, we were never like that with each other."

She looked up at Donovan and saw that he didn't believe her. "We weren't."

"*You* weren't," he corrected. "He would have gone out with you."

Well, she wasn't going to deny that. Tom had asked her out once, but it was right after she'd been hurt badly by another boy and she had told him no. Thank goodness he'd never held it against her.

"Tom's very nice, and he's devoted to his wife," she said, a bit primly.

A laugh escaped Donovan. "All right, I believe you, and he did seem like a great guy."

"You should take him up on his offer. You need some guy time." Donovan didn't answer, so Anna looked up to find him studying her a bit more solemnly than she had expected. "What?"

"You're going to make a great mother," he said quietly.

Her heart lurched. She hoped she would be a good mother, but she was absolutely sure that no matter what Donovan had said, he had been a good, even if often absent, father. His ways with her friends and with Frank showed her that he cared about people. He didn't differentiate between rich and poor. Young as he was, Ben must have known that his father adored him.

"You're missing him a lot today, aren't you?" she said, even though it was the last thing on earth she had planned to say. She gasped.

He placed one finger to her lips. "Don't say you're sorry."

She shook her head. "I didn't even think how that would sound. And with people around to hear, too."

"No one's that close to us," he told her. "Your friends stayed downstairs."

Which only made her feel even more guilty. Her friends had gone beyond the bounds of friendship into matchmaking. Donovan wasn't blind. He would know that, and yet he was still being unfailingly polite.

"Anyway, I *am* missing him a lot today. Ben would have loved this," he told her. "He was crazy about the water, the beach, boats. I think that was part of why Cecily chose a house in Lake Geneva. The first day I drove into town, I couldn't help thinking that he would love riding on one of these boats and yet, until today, I hadn't even ventured near one. I haven't really even gone out on the water. This morning with Frank…well, it was time to do this."

He should have been allowed to do it alone, Anna couldn't help thinking.

Silence crept in. The sun was bright today, the water and the view of the shore with its gorgeous historic homes was stunningly beautiful, but Donovan was here to face a few demons and this couldn't be a pleasant experience for him.

"I should go sit with the girls so you can have some time to yourself." She rose.

He clamped down on her arm. "I'm asking you as a friend, don't go just yet," he said. "Talk to me. Give me the Anna Nowell tour."

She nodded. "All right. That tower that you see is four stories tall. It's part of Black Point Mansion, which was built in 1888."

Donovan let go of her, and she understood. He needed to do this, but it couldn't be easy. Connection with another person, any person, could help. She placed her hand over his and quietly continued with her speech, even though many of the things she was telling him were things he could get from the tour if he listened.

"That's my favorite," she said suddenly, veering away from the standard tour fare.

He turned her hand and rubbed his thumb over her palm, sending a tremor through her. "It's pretty but so are many others. Why this one?"

"It's unabashedly unpretentious," she said, and she wanted to add, *like you,* but she wouldn't. Her friends were trying to set them up. She couldn't do anything that would sound as if she had gotten some foolish ideas into her own head.

"I like that interpretation," he told her with a laugh.

"You're making this much easier for me. I'm enjoying myself. I want you to know that. Now…tell me what you think of the others. You've got a fascinating perspective on things."

So for the remainder of the tour Anna poured out her secret feelings about these stately old buildings. "I've always thought of that one as the playground. See how all the parts kind of turn and fit together in curves and stairs and arches. It looks like a great place to explore."

She continued on in a rush, keeping her voice soft and low and not waiting for Donovan to reply, hoping her mindless chatter was cocooning him without interfering with his thoughts.

When the boat finally docked again, she rose immediately. He stood beside her, towering over her. For a minute she thought he was going to bow over her hand like some gentleman from the Regency era.

"Thank you, Anna," he said, his eyes filled with warmth.

"Was it…okay?" she asked, hoping he knew that she meant his experience and not her performance.

"Yes. It was what I needed. I haven't really said goodbye to him yet, I guess. I think it's going to be a slow, gradual thing. Today was a start. I'm glad you stayed."

He led her downstairs, only reaching out to touch her when she nearly stumbled and then immediately letting her go. When they finally met up with Nan and Paula, both of them were able to act as if the excursion had been just another sightseeing tour.

"You ladies enjoy the rest of your day," he told Anna's friends. "It's been a pleasure seeing you again."

Anna could see that Paula would have liked to stay around and ask questions, but Nan tugged on her arm. "Have to go help my sister. She called me with a work emergency," she said. "I'll call you," she mouthed silently to Anna as the two women turned to walk away.

"You're parked close by?" Donovan asked. "I'll walk you to your car."

"Oh, that's not necessary. Really," Anna said, feeling as if she had reached her limit of being alone with Donovan.

The truth had dawned on her while she was on the boat. She wanted to sit beside him forever. She was in over her head, and her heart was in grave danger of being broken. This time she couldn't even say that he had betrayed her like Brent had. He hadn't. They'd both been painfully honest with each other, and the truth was that they liked and desired each other. They enjoyed being together, but they couldn't ever have more. "It's close," she lied, "and I have things I need to do."

At first she thought Donovan was going to insist on being gallant, but then he told her he would see her back at Morning View. They were about to go their separate ways when the sound of a woman's voice calling Donovan's name made them both turn.

Dana Wellinton was coming down the street. Her stomach was even more rounded than the last time Anna had seen her, but she was still incredibly beautiful.

Rushing up to them, Dana flashed that perfect smile.

"Donovan, you're just the man I've been looking for. Come have coffee with me." She turned as if Donovan would just follow her. Anna assumed most men would, so she gave a brief wave to Donovan and turned back to her car.

"Dana, you remember Anna, don't you?"

Dana stopped walking. She reluctantly turned around. "Oh, yes. She's your housekeeper." Her expression and tone indicated that her view of housekeepers hadn't improved since she and Anna had last met.

"Yes, she is. It's a fascinating, demanding profession. But Anna's also my friend," Donovan said pointedly. "Unfortunately we were just going home, so I'm afraid I'll have to take a rain check on the coffee. It's been nice seeing you again."

"But…"

"I'm sorry," Donovan said.

"But I just heard from someone that your son's birthday would be coming up in a few weeks and I wanted to be the very first to offer you my condolences. You must relive every moment of that accident every day."

Donovan froze in his tracks.

Anna felt her heart turn to stone. She hadn't known. At least she hadn't known the exact date of Ben's birth. No doubt Donovan knew but hadn't wanted to think about it yet. And now he'd been forced to think not only about the fact that Ben wouldn't be here for his birthday but about the horrific way he'd died, just because a selfish woman was trying to score points with him. It was all Anna could do to keep from screaming at Dana.

She wouldn't. She would not make a circus of Donovan's pain in the middle of the street and in front of this insensitive woman.

And yet...Dana seemed confused, even forlorn, clueless. For a minute Anna felt sorry for the woman and her children. Some people just didn't get it, and maybe they were to be pitied. If it weren't for the fact that her words had surely hit Donovan with something he hadn't readied himself for, Anna might have felt a hint of sympathy.

"Thank you, but I have to go," Donovan said, his voice rough, his lips stiff.

He took Anna by the arm and started to lead her away. She knew he had no idea where they were going, but she said nothing until they were out of sight of Dana. Then she stopped. She turned to him.

He glared at her. "If you're thinking of telling me that you're sorry again I warn you I'll be forced to kiss you and keep kissing you until you stop talking," he said, his voice pitched low.

Anna shook her head. "I wasn't going to say that. I was going to say that your son's birthday shouldn't be a cause of condolences. He lived and he made people happy just by being here. His birthday should be a cause for celebration."

Donovan stared down into her eyes, his eyes dark and agonized. Then, without warning, he placed his hands on her arms and pulled her toward him. He drew her close and kissed her. Slowly. Thoroughly. He tasted, he savored, he drove her insane.

Then he let her go and started walking. "You're an amazing woman. It's going to be hard to walk away from you," he said.

But he did. He took her to her car, made sure that she was safely inside and then he walked away.

Anna could barely control her trembling. Donovan's kiss had taken her completely by surprise. It had made her realize just how pathetic she had become where this man was concerned. While he was touching her she hadn't had one thought for anyone else who might have been walking down the street.

Now, however, she worried that someone had seen their embrace. She didn't want anyone to misunderstand him or criticize Donovan for kissing his housekeeper. Mostly, though, she wanted to run after him.

Instead she drove home. She tried not to think about the fact that her friends were trying to pair her up with Donovan. She tried not to think about what she had discovered when Dana had said the words that had ripped Donovan so badly.

But her efforts failed.

I'm in love with him, Anna thought.

And that made staying with Donovan impossible, even if leaving meant putting off her dreams. If she stayed, he would discover the truth. Then he would feel not love but guilt.

That wasn't going to happen, because she was going to leave here and find a new job.

"I will," she whispered to herself, "just as soon as I

can find someone to help him. Someone dependable and honest and…"

Not in love with him, she wanted to add, but she didn't. The truth was that any woman who worked for him would eventually fall in love with him, but not all of them would have children or want children or remind him daily of his loss just by her very existence.

There must be many women who would be perfect for this job, Anna acknowledged. Too bad she was no longer one of them.

The next few days were going to be difficult, but for now…

She began to go through her list of friends and coworkers, searching for someone who would fit.

CHAPTER THIRTEEN

IT WAS late by the time Donovan came home. He'd spent hours pacing, walking the shore path and wondering how he could have behaved so abominably.

He knew Anna desired him just as he desired her, but he also knew that she had grown up here. She cared what people thought. How utterly callous of him to practically maul her on a public street. Her eyes had been shocked when he'd let her go. He owed her so much more...

Beginning with a call explaining why he was late and letting her know he had a few more errands to take care of.

Anna had listened carefully. Her voice had betrayed nothing. Over the phone he couldn't get a handle on how she was feeling, and it drove him nuts. He wanted to be face-to-face with her.

Of course, that was the problem. He wanted to be face-to-face with her all the time these days. He had tried to stay away, tried to keep his hands off her, tried to keep from thinking about her and worrying about her and wanting to be with her. None of it was working.

She deserved a man who would agree to all the babies she wanted, a man who could be a good father and a good husband. She deserved a normal life. Now, not later. Not someday.

Soon he was going to have to leave Lake Geneva. He'd grown to like it here. He was even beginning to feel more like a man and less like a complete disaster, and so much of that was because of Anna and the people she'd brought into his life. But he owed her the chance at a normal life, and she couldn't have that if she kept running into him, a man who was apt to grab her without warning.

Anna would find a man like Tom someday. She would find love, because of course men would love her. Then she would discover that not all men were idiots.

Donovan could barely breathe. His chest felt tight.

"But some men *are* idiots," he muttered. He was one of them. Of course, he had to leave. This was her town, her home, the place where she would find love and raise her babies.

"So do something, Barrett. Finish it. Make her happy," he ordered himself.

He pulled out his telephone and dialed.

Phil picked up on the third ring. "Donovan?" he asked when Donovan had said hello and apologized for calling him at home. "Hey, buddy, don't apologize. I'm glad you felt comfortable doing that. We used to talk all the time."

"I know. I remember. I'm truly sorry I haven't been a better friend," Donovan said suddenly. A part of him wanted to smile. It was the kind of thing Anna would have said.

"Don't," Phil replied. "Maybe *I* wasn't the best of friends. I shouldn't have pushed you when you weren't ready." Donovan could tell that Phil wanted to ask if he was ready now, but his friend refrained.

"I probably would have pushed, too, if our positions had been reversed," Donovan said. "I suppose you know why I'm calling. I wanted to wait, but…"

Phil laughed. "No one wants to wait when adoption is the issue. Actually, I was planning on calling you in a couple of days when things gel a bit more. I've put some feelers out. There are a couple of possibilities." He explained the cases. "I can't promise anything. Nothing is firm as of yet."

Donovan sighed. "That's all right. I haven't told Anna yet, so nothing's firm here, either."

"It's touchy," Phil agreed. "Both sides have to be sure. And everyone has to know the lay of the land going in. These cases can be wonderfully fulfilling and successful, but they also have the potential to be filled with land mines."

"But there's hope for something soon?"

"I think I can say there's an excellent chance. Even if this case doesn't work out, from what you've told me, your Anna sounds like she'd be an exemplary parent. We'll find something, but you have to talk to her, Donovan. I haven't done much beyond asking questions of some colleagues, scouting out possibilities. Without Anna, that's as far as we can go."

"I know. I just wanted to test the waters. I'll get back to you soon." He started to say goodbye.

"Donovan, do you think you'll ever come back?"

Donovan knew that Phil meant more than just to Chicago. He was talking about medicine.

"I don't have any plans right now," he said. "None."

Beyond making sure that Anna had what she needed and wanted. That was the next step. Then he would see to himself.

Anna was trying to keep herself busy the next morning and keep her mind off of Donovan when he showed up in the hallway beside her. She'd been taking inventory of a linen closet even though she already knew exactly what and how much was in the closet.

Turning to meet him, she tried to figure out how to tell him that she was going to leave him without making him feel bad about kissing her and without revealing that she had somehow gone and done something stupid like falling in love with him.

He looked so serious. Staring up into his intense eyes, with his hair falling over his forehead he was like a dark lord ready to tell her that something terrible had happened.

"What?" she asked, not knowing why she asked.

"I need to talk to you. Outside would be best. Seated would definitely be preferable." Gently he took the cloth she was holding and, with her hand in his, he led her out to the deck and beyond. There was a bench midway between the deck and the shore, shaded by a willow. It was private. No one from the house or the shore would hear them here.

Anna wet her lips nervously. She wondered if she

should give him her resignation now along with the list of possible candidates she'd stayed up all night making.

But he surprised her by reaching out and gently smoothing his thumb over her cheek. "You didn't sleep well. You have circles beneath your eyes. That's my fault."

"No," she said, even though it had been him who had kept her awake.

"I'm sorry I kissed you in the middle of the street yesterday. I seem to have made a habit of that. I know it has to stop. Cold turkey this time."

Her heart fell even though he was only telling her what they'd already discussed. "Yes."

"I don't know how much longer I'll be in Lake Geneva," he said quietly. "Not long, I don't think. I came here to get away from things that were destroying me, and I think I've done that. You've helped me. I want to help you before I go. I have connections in Chicago. Private adoption is a possibility. I hope you don't mind but I've made some calls. You could have your baby sooner than you might have thought."

He was leaving. He was leaving. The words ran through her mind and her heart hurt and her eyes ached and she wanted to cry but if she did, she would hurt him. Anna swallowed.

"I can't afford the medical fees."

"I can."

Mutely she shook her head.

"Yes, Anna. Let me."

"I can't take your money."

"You can. You have to."

Don't think about him going. Don't think about anything sad, she ordered herself. "Why?" she managed to say.

He shook his head. "Why do you have to take my money?" He hesitated. "Consider it a severance package. I promised you one once, remember?"

"A severance package couldn't be nearly as much as you're offering," she said. And then she could no longer avoid thinking about what all of this meant. He was going and…

"You're firing me," she said, her voice a whisper. Her heart was breaking at the thought of his leaving, but the other thought—that he was dissatisfied with her—was wrenching her soul apart.

"No." The word was like a shot. Loud. Emphatic. Even angry. "Damn it, no, Anna. I can't believe I gave you that impression. I—"

He leaned forward, cupped her chin and placed a kiss on her cheek. "No." He kissed her forehead. "No. I just want you to be happy."

She couldn't be happy. Donovan was leaving.

"I understand," she said, her voice weakened by the tears she refused to let fall. "You feel bad because you're leaving me without a job. You feel sorry for me."

"That's not it at all." Donovan cupped her face then and forced her to stare into his eyes. "You're a strong, vibrant, admirable woman. I don't feel sorry for you, but your happiness matters to me. More than you know."

His voice was harsh, and Anna felt as if she were somehow making him miserable. She wanted to tell him that his happiness mattered to her, too. That was the only reason she was working to hold her tears back and trying so hard not to beg him to stay. She didn't know how to make any of this right. Taking the money seemed wrong, but if she took it, that might free Donovan. He wouldn't feel guilty. He could leave here satisfied and with no regrets.

"I want you to be happy, too," she said.

He groaned. "Then take the money. Let me help you make your dreams come true."

Anna knew she hadn't earned that money. Taking it didn't even seem honorable, and yet she knew she had to say yes. She could never tell Donovan that he couldn't make all of her dreams come true. She would have her child, and she would be eternally grateful, but she would never have Donovan, the man she now realized she loved more than she had ever loved anyone.

"Anna, please," he said.

A low, whining sound split the air. The sound of a harsh yell and a scream froze Anna's blood. Then a crash, loud and metallic and terrible followed.

She and Donovan turned to each other in shock. The scream had been male. Young. Familiar.

Then Anna ran, with all her might. Her heart screaming, the tears already flowing, Anna turned toward the place where the crash had sounded. Well over a block away. When she made it to the street and had run a full block, Donovan passed her up.

A small sports car sat halfway off the road at a skewed angle, tire tracks showing the path it had taken.

The driver was trying to crawl out the door, but a bicycle, Frank's bicycle, lay partially under the car, up against the door, its frame bent.

Anna scanned the scene, looking for Frank. *Please, please, please be okay,* her mind chanted, even though she knew he couldn't be okay. She couldn't even find him. He'd obviously been thrown.

"Frank!" she cried.

"There," Donovan said, already moving to a small stand of bushes across the road.

Following him, Anna saw what Donovan had seen. A loose tennis shoe, an arm, the small mass that was Frank's body. There was blood. Oh, so much blood. Frank's body was twisted, his legs sprawled, his left arm at an awful angle.

Anna struggled for breath. She fought blackness as she tried to get to Frank.

"He turned out of the driveway like a flash," the driver was saying, limping over. "I didn't see him at first. I tried to swerve. Is he—"

The man didn't finish his sentence, and no one answered him.

Donovan dropped to his knees heavily. He stared at Frank. Then he looked at his own hands.

Anna saw they were shaking. Seconds were ticking away, and fear ripped through her. She didn't know what to do to help Frank.

"Donovan…"

He didn't answer at first.

"Donovan…"

He still didn't look at her.

"Donovan," she begged.

He took a deep, shuddering breath. "Call 911," he said. Then he moved to sit behind Frank's head.

"We're here, Frank," Donovan said, even though Frank hadn't moved. "You've been in an accident, but you're not alone. Help is on the way." His voice was low and almost robotically calm. It betrayed none of the shakiness that Anna had seen in his hands.

"He's breathing. We'll leave the helmet on. It's very important that we not move his head until the EMTs arrive and can stabilize him. His leg is bleeding. I need something to stanch that," Donovan said, looking up at Anna. His eyes were dark, anguished.

Then things started happening very fast. Donovan started barking orders. "Lie down," he told the motorist who was crying and swaying. "If you faint and hit your head, things will be worse. Get off your feet."

The man complied.

Within minutes Donovan had mobilized all of his staff. He had asked for and gotten cloths to stanch the blood flowing from Frank's leg. He had cut away Frank's clothing and examined him, trying to ascertain if there might be any internal injuries. He kept Frank's head immobilized, continuing to check his vitals.

Anna was vaguely aware of a murmuring, of the sound of neighbors and bypassers gathering, stopping to stare. But her heart and her mind were on the man and boy in front of her. Donovan was dark-eyed and tense, completely focused on what was happening beneath his hands. And Frank was lying so still. Too still? Was this as bad as it looked?

Anna bit her lip. The thought of Frank never smiling again, never being…here was too terrible to even consider. And the prospect of Donovan losing a child he'd tried to save after what he'd been through…Anna's heart felt like a bird trying to flutter its way out of her chest. She felt sick. So very sick. Perhaps she swayed.

"Don't do that. Don't lose it on me, sweetheart." Donovan's voice reached her. "Talk to him, Anna. Softly. Sing to him, hum to him. We can't tell if he can hear or not, but he may be able to. If so, it might help."

Anna talked; she sang. She told Frank a story about the first time she met him. She watched Donovan working over his patient and casting fleeting glances toward the driver in the grass.

Once, when the man groaned, Donovan looked down at his hands as if he wished that he had more than one pair. There were people around, some who were talking to the driver but none who appeared to know what to do if the man warranted medical attention. Anna could see the agitation in the glances Donovan gave the man, but he never left Frank. Frank who was so pale that he looked almost—

She couldn't even think it. Anyway, it wasn't true. He was breathing. Donovan was checking his pulse, touching his skin to see if shock had set in.

"Stay with me, Anna," Donovan said. She did. She kept talking to Frank.

Sirens sounded in the distance. Donovan spared a

glance for his watch. He'd done it before. She knew what he was thinking. Getting trauma patients transported to a hospital quickly was of incredible importance. The Platinum Ten Minutes. She'd seen it on a news program.

"Donovan," she began, but then Frank stirred and whimpered.

"Son, can you tell me your name?" Donovan whispered urgently. "Don't try to move your head. Don't try to nod. Just talk to me. Tell me your name," he said as Frank's parents drove up in their car and ran over to their son.

Anna nodded to them. They looked so lost. They nodded back and moved away slightly to let Donovan take care of their child. Anna noticed that Donovan didn't look at them. His concentration was completely on Frank.

"Can you tell me your name?" he coaxed again.

"I—yes." When Frank managed both first and last names in a raspy, disjointed voice, Donovan closed his eyes.

Immediately he opened them again. He looked directly at Anna as he asked Frank a few more questions. For a few seconds it felt as if all three of them were connected, Anna couldn't help thinking. But now that Frank was coming to, he was in pain and he was scared. He started to buck.

"Frank," Donovan said. "I know you hurt, but don't move."

"I—Donovan, my arm—"

"I've got you, buddy," Donovan's voice soothed like

cool medicine. "The ambulance is on the way. Better than a bike, even. A big, fast, red car? You'll be the talk of the school."

Frank stared at Donovan, his eyes glazed but completely trusting. Anna's heart flipped.

"Okay, big guy. The ambulance is almost here," Donovan said as the sirens grew louder. "You hang on and lie still and we're going to take you out of here. These guys tend to be very good. They know their stuff, and they're fast, too."

His words were low. He continued to monitor Frank, but he was so unobtrusive about it that Anna doubted Frank was even aware that Donovan was tracking every beat of his heart and every breath he took.

"Frank?"

"Yes?"

"What day is it?"

"Wednesday."

"You got it. Where are we?"

Frank started to try to shake his head. Donovan soothed him, leaning close to whisper encouragement.

"By Anna's," Frank whispered back. He moaned.

"You're doing great, Frank. That was an excellent job. Keep holding on and listening to me. What kind of sports do you play?"

"Baseball," Frank managed to say, his voice thick.

"Pitcher?"

"Catcher." She knew what he was doing. Trying to monitor Frank for shock and trying to keep the boy's mind off his pain and fear.

The exchange only lasted a moment. The emergency vehicles arrived. Donovan and the emergency workers moved into action, getting Frank on a cot, his neck in a brace. They put him in the ambulance and Frank's mother climbed in.

Anna rushed to Donovan who was starting to look ragged around the edges now that he was no longer the sole person in charge. She wanted to ask if Frank would be all right, but she couldn't ask that of Donovan. If the answer was no…

He was getting ready to climb into the ambulance.

"I'll meet you at the hospital," she said.

Donovan stopped. "Have someone drive you."

She opened her mouth to protest. "Anna, please. You're upset and…if you're not careful…"

"I'll have someone drive me," she promised. She would not argue this time, and she wouldn't cause Donovan to worry about her as well as Frank. He'd had too many personal experiences with auto accidents and their victims.

As he moved into the ambulance, the commanding presence he had been for the past few minutes seemed to disappear. His shoulders sagged. He looked beaten. He hesitated for just a second. Then he took a visible breath, squared his shoulders and moved in to see to Frank.

Hours later, at the hospital, after Anna had talked to a woozy Frank and found out that Frank had suffered a mild concussion, had a broken arm, several gashes and cuts and many bruises along with a broken rib, but that he would be back on his bike in time, Anna finally felt as if she could breathe.

People had been coming and going the entire time she was here. So many people knew and cared about Frank. Tom had shown up. He'd pressed a copy of a flier into her hands.

"They were handing these out at the office. Frank is on the school paper and even though it's summer, some of the kids managed to get a notice out about Frank's accident. Everyone was worried about him, and this seemed like a good way to pass the news along."

Anna read the copy, its words bringing tears to her eyes.

"Thank you," she told Tom.

"I thought the Doc might want to read it," he said, looking a bit sheepish. "Hey, it's only a school rag, but how often do you make the papers?"

It was a lame excuse, but Anna was grateful. She clutched the piece of paper and made her way to a room where one of the interns had told her that Dr. Barrett was resting. The door was open, so she slid inside.

Donovan was on a couch, his big body taking up the whole space. He lay on his side, his lashes resting on his cheeks. Even with his eyes closed, he looked exhausted. He looked wonderful, Anna thought.

She stepped forward. The temptation to just stand here and watch him breathe was too much for her. She took another step. A hand reached out and looped around her wrist. She gasped and looked into Donovan's eyes.

He started to sit up.

"No, don't," she said. "You're tired."

He ignored her and sat up anyway.

"You should be home," he told her.

"You, too."

He shrugged. "I heard that Frank is going to be fine," she told him.

"I know. I'm…glad." His voice was thick with emotion.

"You were pretty wonderful, you know."

Donovan frowned. He looked down at his hands as if he didn't know what they were and then he looked at Anna. "I didn't save him, Anna. He would have survived had I not been there."

"Not everyone feels that way." She held out the flier. It was a childish recounting of how Frank had been hit by a car and how Donovan Barrett had saved his life. She explained why Frank's friends had written the missive. "You're a hero to them," she said.

"Go home, Anna," he said wearily.

She shook her head.

"Anna, I balked. I froze. When we heard that crash, I knew it was Frank. You ran. I didn't. For a good ten seconds, maybe more, I didn't even move. And when I got to the scene, I couldn't do a thing. My hands were like stones. My mind wouldn't function. At all. If you hadn't called my name, if you hadn't been there, if the situation had been worse…"

He shoved one hand back though his hair. "Go home, Anna."

"Donovan, I—"

"No. Don't."

She looked into his eyes and knew there was nothing she could say. Her mind was screaming at her to say something, do something, to stop the tragedy that was happening.

Donovan was drawing back into himself. He was telling her that he had failed Frank, but she didn't think that was the whole of it. More likely, he wasn't seeing Frank lying on the street, but Ben, while Donovan froze and let him die.

"Come home," she said. She touched his arm. She lay a hand on his chest.

Donovan sucked in a deep breath and then he grasped her. He pulled her against him, resting his chin on top of her head.

"I can't be what you need me to be, Anna. And I won't be anything less. Go home, sweetheart."

Anna's heart broke on the endearment. Donovan was at it again. Protecting her. As he'd protected Frank, even as he'd protected the man who had hit Frank, by making the man lie down and remain still. Anna was equally sure that Donovan had given pieces of his soul to many people, trying to help them, to save them.

He'd probably even lost a time or two, but he'd kept trying…until Ben's death had turned everything inside out.

"I'm no hero," he whispered.

She nodded. "You don't have to be." She kissed him. But she knew he was so very wrong. He was *her* hero. He had been from the word go. But he wouldn't want to hear that. She didn't intend to tell him.

A chasm stood between her and the man she loved. One that seemed impossible to bridge. It had always been there. She had always accepted it. But as she'd watched Donovan with Frank today, as she'd seen him doing the work he'd been born to do, she'd learned something. Or maybe she'd simply opened her eyes to something she'd already known.

Life would always be full of dangers, frightening situations, the possibility of failure or even death. But if a person didn't try, failure was a given. Death would win. Life had no chance. Donovan could have walked away from the accident and simply waited for someone else to take charge. He'd probably wanted to, but like it or not, he wasn't built that way. People like Donovan gave life a chance, and even if they sometimes lost, the fact that they tried mattered.

She couldn't blame Donovan for quitting his practice. He'd lost the ultimate. He'd lost a child. He'd outlived his baby. That was a life-changing situation. It made trying so much harder, seemingly impossible.

And yet…when it had counted, when there had been only him or no one to help, he had tried. He had given. If he found himself in that same situation again, he would do it again. Because of Ben, it would hurt. Ben would always be the one he hadn't been able to help, but in the end he would still do what needed doing.

Anna took a deep breath and thought about where that left her. The chasm, the distance between herself and Donovan. She'd thought it was impassable, but just as there would always be chasms in life, there would always be bridge builders, too. Without people making an attempt to cross over, the chasm would remain forever.

Right now Donovan was on an island, separated from her and from life. What he needed was a bridge builder.

Anna closed her eyes. What if she failed?

She could damage him.

But he was already damaged. If she didn't try, he would be alone forever on his island.

Anna picked up the phone. She said goodbye to her dreams and prayed for hope.

CHAPTER FOURTEEN

DONOVAN was alone in the library. He was making lists of things that had to be done before he left Lake Geneva. And he had to leave. He was hurting Anna. He could see it in her eyes.

He had disrupted her life when all she had ever wanted was a child. Now she was worrying about him. That had been clear at the hospital yesterday.

Her friends were trying to match her up with him. He'd known that and he'd allowed it to go on, even encouraged it when he'd known he had nothing to offer a woman like Anna.

You love her. The words seemed to sizzle in the air. He couldn't deny them. He loved Anna. Desperately. He'd told her he wasn't a hero, and he wasn't. Only years of experience had kept him going yesterday when he'd thought Frank's life might hang in the balance. Yet he wanted to be a hero for her.

She needed a hero. She needed a child.

He intended to see that she got at least one of those.

It was time to talk to Phil again and set things in motion at last.

The sound of the doorbell ringing broke into his thoughts. Anna was somewhere in the house, but the doorbell rang again. And again.

"She must be outside," he muttered, amazed that he didn't know exactly where she was. Ever since he'd come here he'd been constantly aware of her. The fact that he didn't feel her presence now made it seem as if a piece of him was missing. She had to be outside.

He swung the door open. A couple was standing on the doorstep. He recognized the woman as Frank's mother.

"Come in," he said, motioning them inside.

The man shuffled his feet, looking slightly uncomfortable, even as he stepped over the threshold. "Thank you. Okay." He held a baseball cap in his hands and was twisting it around and around. "We just…we wanted to thank you."

Donovan froze. He frowned and opened his mouth.

"Don't say you didn't do anything," the woman said. "Anna told me that you were denying that you made a difference, but, Dr. Barrett, we were there. Frank was really busted up. Maybe it wasn't life or death, but it felt like it at the time. You cared, and you knew what you were doing. We could see that. Everyone could see it. Frank was afraid and hurting. You calmed him. You calmed us. You can't know how much that meant."

Anna walked in, then. She was accompanied by a man. Donovan recognized him as one of the EMTs from the other day. "Dr. Barrett," he said. "I just wanted to tell you that it was an honor working alongside you yesterday. Most of the time, it's just me and my crew, and we're usually there in a heartbeat, but it was a bad day for accidents and we were running a couple of minutes slower than I would have liked. I can't tell you how glad I was to see that someone already had things in hand. Anna tells me that you had quite a reputation in Chicago, but I would never have known it."

Donovan blinked and the man turned red. "By that, I mean that you didn't get all high-handed just because you're a Chicago physician. You helped us do our job and you *let* us do our job without throwing your weight around. I'd be happy to work with you again."

"I—" Donovan didn't know what to say. "Thank you. Same here." He shook the man's hand. Now was not the time to tell the man he had hung up his stethoscope for good.

Anna smiled and spoke quietly to the man, leading him into the kitchen where Frank's parents were already ensconced. It seemed that there was a buffet in the kitchen.

"What's this about?" Donovan asked Anna.

"It's about truth," she said. "It's about heroes."

He frowned. "I told you—"

She placed her hand over his mouth, then replaced her fingers with her lips. "I know what you told me. But today I want you to listen, to hear, the way you used to hear your patients. You were known as a sympathetic doctor. I know. I've looked up everything I could find about you in the newspapers, on the Internet, in blogs."

"You're kidding, right. Blogs?"

"Well…I might have posed a question or two. Someone might have written an oratory about you as a result. Your patients and their families loved you, Donovan. Let that happen here."

"I can't do that again, Anna. I can't try to be a hero."

"Then don't be. You don't have to be that if you don't want to. Just be an ordinary man, one who cares. Because you do care. Be a doctor who uses his skills. Because you do have skills. Ones that make a difference."

He didn't know what to say to that. Anna was looking up at him, her eyes shining. And he couldn't help himself. He kissed her. "I care. Very much," he said.

"I know." She smiled again. He knew she didn't understand that he was talking about his feelings for her, not general feelings about the world or his former patients.

But he lost his chance to tell her. A steady stream of people began to file through his house. Parents. Frank's friends. People who had been there on the roadside watching that day. The man who had been driving the sports car.

"You gave me hope when I was half out of my mind," he told Donovan.

"I want my baby to have a doctor like you," a pregnant woman said.

A man and woman with a little girl came up. "You helped Frankie," the little girl said. "Frankie's my friend."

Another little boy tugged on his sleeve. "Frankie says you have a cool car."

Donovan couldn't help grinning. "You like cool cars?"

"Yup."

He ended up taking the boy out to the garage. People streamed out of the house, the men and many of the women exclaiming over Donovan's cool car, others strolling through his gardens.

"Thank you for being there," some said. "Thank you for having us here." They came; they smiled; they talked; they ate; they began to file out.

"Welcome to the area," one elderly woman said, taking Donovan's hand as she readied herself to leave. "I live in Chicago. I've heard of you. I know your reputation and I know what I saw the other day. You were given a gift. Not just the gift of healing, but the gift of caring and of soothing those who are hurting. It's a difficult job, I don't doubt that, but…to walk away from the gift…please don't. We need people like you."

Donovan felt his throat tighten. The woman was smiling at him. He remembered all the people who had come through here today. He remembered Frank. He remembered his patients back in Chicago…and Ben. Could he have saved Ben had he been there? He didn't know. He would never know, but standing here today, he realized this much. He could help some people, save some children. Not all, but some.

It was a truth he had been hiding from. He looked around, trying to find Anna. Damn woman. She wouldn't leave a man alone. She never had. Thank goodness.

Donovan smiled at the woman who had been talking to him. He thanked her. He took a deep breath and faced the rest of the truth.

The road back to life was going to be painful and

scary, and he might need time to ease back in, but he saw now that he couldn't really back away. He'd tried and he'd failed to quit. That was something to think about.

Then, suddenly, the last person left. The room went quiet. Donovan and Anna were alone. She'd been smiling at him all day but now she looked nervous. Tense. Uncertain. She walked across the floor, away from him, her heels clicking on the marble.

"Why?" he asked, but she didn't turn around.

He went to her, slid his arms around her and turned her to face him. She looked down. He placed a finger under her chin and tilted her face up to look at him.

"Why did I invade your privacy and force you into a position like this?" she asked.

He smiled. "Maybe the question I should ask is how? How did you know that I needed this? How did you know that it was inevitable that I would go back to medicine, that I couldn't walk away?"

She bit her lip. She took a deep breath. "Because I know you. Because I love you."

He closed his eyes, tightening his hold on her, pulling her so close that she was almost a part of his body. His lips came down on hers. "You wonderful, crazy, stubborn, amazing woman."

"It's all right that you don't love me," she said. "The truth is that, like it or not, what I saw yesterday was…you need to be a doctor. You could never walk away from an injured child. That's not the way you're made. And I—I just wanted you to have what you needed."

Donovan pulled back. "And you know what I need?"

She nodded slowly. "Yes. To go back to Chicago and take up your practice again."

Anna stared up at Donovan, her heart both rejoicing and breaking at the same time. Donovan was going to have some semblance of happiness and sanity and serenity again. He was going to be a doctor once more. She was pretty sure of that.

And she? She was going to lose him forever. She tried to keep smiling. Why had she admitted that she loved him? Because it was the truth and because it was, indeed, why she understood his needs.

His eyes were dark. He swept her closer. "What if you're what I need, Anna? What if I love you?"

Her heart beat faster. She placed her hands on his chest and tried to read his expression.

"You don't. Desire isn't love."

"No," he agreed. "It isn't, and I do desire you. But I've loved you from the day I met you, even if I didn't want to admit it. How could I not? You stirred up my world, drove me crazy and insisted on doing what was best for me. I came here, recklessly running from my life and ran right into you. It was the luckiest day of my life, Anna."

Donovan brought his lips down on hers. He tasted, he took, he gave back everything until Anna was shaking so hard she could barely stand.

Leading her to a sofa in the sunroom that overlooked the lake, Donovan pulled her close. "I've been running away for too long," he said. "Now I want to run to something. To you, Anna. Love me. Marry me?"

"You can't be sure." She frowned.

He smiled. "I'm positive. I don't want to live without you in my life."

She smiled up at him. "Yes, but…"

Alarm flashed in his eyes. "But what?"

She leaned closer. "I don't have to have a child. I don't want you to worry about that."

"It's been your dream."

"My dream was to have someone to love unconditionally." She kissed him again.

When she pulled back, he was smiling. "I think we have enough love to spare for a child."

"You don't have to do that."

He shook his head. "When Frank was hurt, a part of me knew that I couldn't hold back and still help him. I couldn't shield my heart without freezing up. And you know something? I dreamed of Ben last night. Maybe it was because his birthday was near and you told me that it should be celebrated. Maybe it was because of what happened yesterday, but…he was smiling. And I think Ben would have loved Frank, too. He would be glad I was with him in the ambulance. If they were the same age they might have become friends. So, I'm betting my son will understand that I'll never stop loving him even if I have other children to love."

"He loves you still. And always," she told him. "It flows from heaven to your heart and back again."

Donovan's kiss was gentle, reverent. "You had dreams when I met you."

"I still do. You're in every one of them."

"You've taught me how to dream again. And I do. Of you. Every day," he said, kissing her eyes. "Every night." He kissed her nose. "Sweet dreams," he said as he kissed her on the mouth.

Anna smiled up at him. "Donovan, do you realize you're kissing your housekeeper again? What will people say?" she teased.

"I imagine they'll say that I'm a very lucky man," he told her, amusement lighting his eyes.

"You're a wonderful man, my love," she said.

Then neither of them said anything more, for she was in his arms and that was all that mattered.

* * * * *

Turn the page for a sneak preview of
IF I'D NEVER KNOWN YOUR LOVE
by
Georgia Bockoven

From the brand-new series
Harlequin Everlasting Love
Every great love has a story to tell.™

There's no way for you to know this, Evan, but I haven't written to you for a few months. Actually, it's been almost a year. I had a hard time picking up a pen once more after we paid the second ransom and then received a letter saying it wasn't enough. I was so sure you were coming home that I took the kids along to Bogotá so they could fly home with you and me, something I swore I'd never do. I've fallen in love with Colombia and the people who've opened their hearts to me. But fear is a constant companion when I'm there. I won't ever expose our children to that kind of danger again.

I'm at a loss over what to do anymore, Evan. I've begged and pleaded and thrown temper tantrums with every official I can corner both here and at home. They've been incredibly tolerant and understanding, but in the end as ineffectual as the rest of us.

I try to imagine what your life is like now, what you do every day, what you're wearing, what you eat. I want to believe that the people who have you are misguided yet kind, that they treat you well. It's how I survive day to day. To think of you being mistreated hurts too much. If I picture you locked away somewhere and suffering, a weight descends on me that makes it almost impossible to get out of bed in the morning.

Your captors surely know you by now. They have to recognize what a good man you are. I imagine you working with their children, telling them that you have children, too, showing them the pictures you carry in your wallet. Can't the men who have you understand how much your children miss you? How can it not matter to them?

How can they keep you away from us all this time? Over and over, we've done what they asked. Are they oblivious to the depth of their cruelty? What kind of people are they that they don't care?

I used to keep a calendar beside our bed next to the peach rose you picked for me before you left. Every night I marked another day, counting how many you'd been gone. I don't do that any longer. I don't want to be reminded of all the days we'll never get back.

When I can't sleep at night, I tell you about my day. I imagine you hearing me and smiling over the details that make up my life now. I never tell you how defeated I feel at moments or how hard I work to hide it from everyone for fear they will see it as a reason to stop believing you are coming home to us.

And I couldn't tell you about the lump I found in my breast and how difficult it was going through all the tests without you here to lean on. The lump was benign—the process reaching that diagnosis utterly terrifying. I couldn't stop thinking about what would happen to Shelly and Jason if something happened to me.

We need you to come home.

I'm worn down with missing you.

I'm going to read this tomorrow and will probably tear it up or burn it in the fireplace. I don't want you to get the idea I ever doubted what I was doing to free you or thought the work a burden. I would gladly spend the rest of my life at it, even if, in the end, we only had one day together.

You are my life, Evan.

I will love you forever.

* * * * *

*Don't miss this deeply moving Harlequin Everlasting
Love story about a woman's struggle to bring back
her kidnapped husband from Colombia and her
turmoil over whether to let go, finally, and welcome
another man into her life.
IF I'D NEVER KNOWN YOUR LOVE
by Georgia Bockoven
is available March 27, 2007.*

*And also look for THE NIGHT WE MET
by Tara Taylor Quinn, a story about finding love
when you least expect it.*

REQUEST YOUR FREE BOOKS!
2 FREE NOVELS PLUS 2
FREE GIFTS!

H A R L E Q U I N   R O M A N C E®

From the Heart, For the Heart

YES! Please send me 2 FREE Harlequin Romance® novels and my 2 FREE gifts. After receiving them, if I don't wish to receive any more books, I can return the shipping statement marked "cancel." If I don't cancel, I will receive 4 brand-new novels every month and be billed just $3.57 per book in the U.S., or $4.05 per book in Canada, plus 25¢ shipping and handling per book and applicable taxes, if any*. That's a savings of over 15% off the cover price! I understand that accepting the 2 free books and gifts places me under no obligation to buy anything. I can always return a shipment and cancel at any time. Even if I never buy another book from Harlequin, the two free books and gifts are mine to keep forever.

114 HDN EEV7 314 HDN EEWK

Name _____ (PLEASE PRINT)

Address _____ Apt. _____

City _____ State/Prov. _____ Zip/Postal Code _____

Signature (if under 18, a parent or guardian must sign)

Mail to the **Harlequin Reader Service®**:
IN U.S.A.: P.O. Box 1867, Buffalo, NY 14240-1867
IN CANADA: P.O. Box 609, Fort Erie, Ontario L2A 5X3

Not valid to current Harlequin Romance subscribers.

Want to try two free books from another line?
Call 1-800-873-8635 or visit www.morefreebooks.com.

* Terms and prices subject to change without notice. NY residents add applicable sales tax. Canadian residents will be charged applicable provincial taxes and GST. This offer is limited to one order per household. All orders subject to approval. Credit or debit balances in a customer's account(s) may be offset by any other outstanding balance owed by or to the customer. Please allow 4 to 6 weeks for delivery.

Your Privacy: Harlequin is committed to protecting your privacy. Our Privacy Policy is available online at www.eHarlequin.com or upon request from the Reader Service. From time to time we make our lists of customers available to reputable firms who may have a product or service of interest to you. If you would prefer we not share your name and address, please check here. ☐

HR07

Coming Next Month

#3943 RAISING THE RANCHER'S FAMILY Patricia Thayer
Rocky Mountain Brides

New York tycoon Holt Rawlins is back home in Destiny to find the truth, not to make friends. But when beautiful Leah Keenan bursts into his life, Holt finds he cannot let her go. Leah knows that soon she will have to return to her old life, but to leave Holt will break her heart. Will the rugged rancher persuade her to stay?

#3944 MATRIMONY WITH HIS MAJESTY Rebecca Winters
By Royal Appointment

Darrell Collier is an ordinary single mom. Alexander Valleder is a good, responsible king. But one night, years ago, he rebelled a little. The result, as he's just discovered, was a child. Now Alex has to sweep Darrell off her feet and persuade her that she has the makings of a queen.

#3945 THE SHEIKH'S RELUCTANT BRIDE Teresa Southwick
Desert Brides

Jessica Sterling has just discovered that in the desert kingdom of Bha'Khar is the man that she has been betrothed to since birth! Sheikh Kardhal Hourani is rich, gorgeous and arrogant. Can Jessica see the man behind the playboy persona and find her way into his guarded heart?

#3946 IN THE HEART OF THE OUTBACK... Barbara Hannay

Byrne Drummond has every reason to hate Fiona McLaren—her reckless brother destroyed his family. But the image of Byrne has been etched in Fiona's mind ever since she first saw the stoic, broad-shouldered cattleman. And Fiona's touch is the first to draw him in years.

#3947 MARRIAGE FOR BABY Melissa McClone

Career-driven couple Jared and Katie have separated. But when they find themselves guardians of an orphaned baby they agree to give their marriage another go for the sake of the child. Little do they know how much this tiny baby will turn their lives—and marriage—upside down.

#3948 RESCUED: MOTHER-TO-BE Trish Wylie
Baby on Board

Colleen McKenna knew that she would have to be strong to cope with her pregnancy alone. But now gorgeous millionaire Eamonn Murphy's kindness is testing her fierce independence. And having Eamonn share each tiny kick with her makes each moment more special than the last.

EVERLASTING LOVE™

Every great love has a story to tell™

Available March 27

And look for
***The Marriage Bed* by Judith Arnold**
and
***Family Stories* by Tessa Mcdermid,**
from Harlequin® Everlasting Love™
this May.

*If you're a romantic at heart, you'll definitely
want to read this new series. Pick up a book today!*

www.eHarlequin.com

HELAPR07

How do you make yourself needed by a man who only wants to be alone?

Anna Nowell loves her job—living rent-free in a fabulous mansion for an absentee landlord has perks she'd never imagined. But when her boss returns, her dream [illegible] unless Anna can convince him she's i[illegible]

Wealthy, cultured Donovan Barrett was a renowned physician until the tragic death of his son. Grief-stricken, he craves solitude. Consorting with the help isn't on his agenda, but Anna, with her compassion and laughter, has a way of changing all his plans *and* bringing him back to life when he thought he'd never love again….

Harlequin Romance®
www.eHarlequin.com

ISBN-13: 978-0-373-03938-8
ISBN-10: 0-373-03938-7

03938

0 65373 01002 5 UPC

HARLEQUIN® Romance®

From the Heart.
For the Heart.